The Joy of Words

A Collection of Short Stories

P J Harvey

Ark Press

First Published in 2021 by Ark Press

www.philipjharvey.co.uk

The Joy of Words is dedicated to *Farrah Silver*. For the gift of friendship.

Introduction

We all love a good story. Unfortunately, not all of us can find the time to sit down and read. Most of us, in fact, are thankful if we manage to grab a few minutes at the end of the day.

The stories presented in this book have all been written with those precious few minutes in mind.

The first section of the book contains a collection of Sketch Stories. Despite containing fewer than 200 words each, I hope you'll find something to enjoy in all of them.

The next section, entitled Flash Fiction, contains a selection of very short stories. Though longer than the stories presented in the Sketch Stories section, none should take more than five minutes to complete.

The last section contains short stories of a more traditional length, for when life is gracious enough to grant you a little more reading time.

Hopefully, the Sketch Stories and Flash Fiction sections will have left you eager to begin reading these longer works of fiction.

I've included a varied selection of stories in the hopes that everyone will find something to suit, be it a modern-day tale of woe or a medieval mystery.

If you come across a story in a genre you don't particularly enjoy, try it anyway. You might just surprise yourself.

By the time you've finished reading this book, I hope you'll be inspired to make reading a part of your everyday journey.

Perhaps some of you may even put pen to paper, or fingers to the keyboard, and come up with a few stories of your own. Like me, I'm sure you have a few tales to tell.

Sketch Stories

Stupid Fears

Something landed on the duvet and crawled up my leg. Heart pounding, I leapt from the bed and bounded over to the light switch.

The family cat yawned, stretched, circled, dropped back down to the bed.

"Stupid cat."

My limbs still shaking, I slipped back under the duvet.

The light stayed on.

Rusty

Rusty was gorgeous, long black hair, blue eyes, intelligent. He was a runner. He adored kids.

Before he spoke, I knew he was the one for me.

We spent fourteen wonderful years together with never a cross word.

Now I have Buster, a border collie. He's gorgeous too, but he'll never replace my Rusty.

Checkmate

He'd beaten me again. I wasn't surprised. He beat me at everything. It was a competition thing we had.

We often spoke about death. I was ten years older than him. We used to joke that I'd beat him at that. Now he has cancer, so I guess maybe he'll beat me at that too.

Somewhere In Between

I was born on Friday 16th April 1965, at 2.16 pm, a rainy afternoon in spring.

I died on Tuesday 23rd July 2019, at 8.05 am, a gloriously sunny morning in summer.

Somewhere in between, I had a life.

I wish I'd paid more attention to it.

8:00 am

The alarm clock startled me out of my dream.

I wrenched back the curtain and glared at the clock. It told me what I already knew.

It was 6:00 am.

Time to get up.

"Just five more minutes," I told myself.

Five minutes later, I rolled over and looked at the clock.

It was 8:00 am.

The White Room

Three days ago, I spoke to a fairy about her magical dust.

The day after, I spoke to a leprechaun about his pot of gold.

Yesterday, I spoke to a psychiatrist about my condition.

Today, I spoke to four white walls.

Tomorrow?

Tomorrow, I think I'll stop talking, and listen instead to the conversations going on inside my head.

Muse

"Who are you?" I ask.

"Your muse."

I nod. He's seen better days. "Do you have anything for me today?"

"Only what you're writing now. It isn't very good."

He's right. The truth is, I haven't written anything worth reading in over a month.

"What about tomorrow?" I ask.

"Tomorrow looks good," the muse says. "Yes, definitely tomorrow."

He goes back to sleep.

He doesn't wake up.

Father's Day

My dad used to work at a pickle factory in North Carolina. He met Mum at a disco in Illinois. He'd always wanted to drive through St. Louis. I never knew.

I regret having to read this from his diary. I wish I'd known him better when he was alive.

Today, I'm driving through St. Louis.

Anything

"Who are you?"

"Who would you like me to be?"

"I'm really not sure. A friend would be nice."

"I can be that."

"I need someone who'll always be there for me, someone who'll care for me, fight for me."

"I can do all of those things. The truth is, I can be anything you want me to be."

"You can?"

"Of course. You just have to let me."

I sigh. There's always a catch.

"How do I do that?"

"You first have to find me. It's not always easy, but I'll always be here."

Paris

"What should I wear?"

"Try the blue dress," Sam said.

Her wife shouted down the stairs. "What blue dress?"

"The one I got you in Paris."

"But darling, we haven't been to Paris."

Sam choked on her bagel.

Ah hell, that must have been the other wife.

Pictures Don't Lie

Jerry pulled the crumbled picture from his pocket. It showed him arm in arm with his ex-wife.

She was smiling.

He looked happy.

That must have been the day their divorce had come through.

Nowhere to Hide

I know they'll find me. It's just a matter of time.

I'm crouched behind the laundry basket in the cupboard under the stairs. My heart is thumping, the blood pounding in my ears.

I can hear them laughing as they search through the cupboards upstairs.

"She's not under the bed," I hear one of them shout.

"Did you check the cupboard under the stairs?"

My heart skips a beat.

The game's over. There's nowhere to run.

Heavy feet pound the stairs.

Slowly, the door swings open and two grinning faces peer inside.

"Found you." Danny, my youngest, screams in delight. "Now, it's our turn to hide."

"Fine," I say, "just one more game."

Danny grins.

I must have said this ten times already.

Abducted by Aliens

Jerry has lipstick on his collar.

"Where've you been?" I ask.

"You wouldn't believe me."

He's probably right. "Tell me anyway."

"Okay. Fine. I was abducted."

"Abducted?"

"By aliens."

I bite my lip and hold back a sigh. "Aliens?"

Jerry gets undressed and slides into the bed beside me. "I said you wouldn't believe me."

I turn over and turn off the light. "Who said I didn't believe you?"

The darkness is silent.

Ten minutes later . . .

"What? That's it? No interrogation?"

"What? I said I believed you." I roll over and puff up my pillow. "It just so happens that I was abducted by aliens too."

The Gift

I'm sitting outside a coffee shop with my best friend, Sheila. We try to meet at least once a week.

She slides a gift, wrapped in purple tissue paper, across the laminate table.

"I'm sorry, it really isn't much."

I unwrap the present and discover a beautiful beaded necklace. I'm touched that she took the time to make it. I know how busy she is.

"Next year," she says, "next year, I'll buy you something nice."

"You really don't have to," I tell her. "You've already given me so much."

She frowns as she stares at the necklace.

I smile and say, "I'm talking about your friendship. It's a gift I get to unwrap every day."

There are tears in her eyes as our hands clasp across the table. It's wonderful knowing that our friendship means as much to her too.

The Joy of Words

The radio's on, but I haven't heard a single snippet of conversation, can't recall a single song that's been played. I'm too engrossed in my book.

I continue reading, skipping a few words here, a paragraph without dialogue there, eager to find out what happens next.

Then I turn the page and discover I've reached the end of the chapter. I'll have to read more if I'm to find the answers I seek.

I glance at the clock.

It's already past midnight and I've got work in the morning. However, the words call to me louder than sleep.

I lean forward and prop up my pillow. Just one more chapter, I say to myself.

Liar

The door opened, and a shaft of light entered the room.

"What do you want?" Ally asked.

The door closed, and she felt him move to her side of the bed. "I thought you might like to talk."

"About what?"

"Whatever's troubling you."

A hand lightly touched her shoulder, and she pulled away. "Who said I was troubled?"

"Come off it, Ally. This is me you're talking to. I always know when you're lying."

"It's not important. Besides, I don't want to keep troubling you with my problems."

"Maybe I like trouble," he said, "maybe I don't have enough troubles of my own."

She turned and stared at him, forcing back a smile. "Now who's lying?"

He shrugged and gave a wan smile. "I guess neither of us turned out to be very good liars."

Extinguishing the Flame

She placed the candle on the dining room table and stood in front of the mirror.

Nothing had changed. The scar was still visible, a deep, jagged line, cutting a roving path across her face.

She stared into the lifeless eyes and realised nothing of the old her remained. He'd extinguished her flame.

She tried to smile, but the skin pulled tightly against the stitches, turning it instead into a lopsided grin. The satisfaction, she realised, had come too late for it to matter.

Stepping over the body on the floor, she glanced briefly at the blood-soaked knife before moving to the table.

Then, catching the wick between her fingers, she extinguished the flame.

Loss

Jimmy scrambled up onto the old stone wall and peered over the railings into the churchyard.

Hundreds of graves dotted the overgrown cemetery. Some were simple slabs of carved stone displaying recognizable names and dates. Others had raised beds of white marble filled with glass pebbles. Still others, with dates long passed living memory, lay all but forgotten upon the broken ground.

Jimmy sighed and clambered over the railings.

Somewhere, amongst that jumbled mass of stone, lie his mother's grave.

Sleep

A blinding flash rent the sky, immediately followed by the clash of thunder.

The woman breathed the heavy air and clenched a fist to her temple. The dramatic change in weather had brought about the worst kind of headache.

She pushed the twisted sheets to the end of the bed and cast a bleary gaze around the room, then peered out the window, where the night sky blazed with light.

A low boom rattled the window.

Moments later, rain rent its fury on the ground, impacting like explosive shells upon the hard baked earth. It brought with it a relief from the humid air.

Sleep once again beckoned.

Hate

I hate that I look for every convenient shadow on the street, that my hand, worn like a mask, is but an extension of the shadow. I hate that I cannot meet a stranger's gaze for fear of seeing the source of the easy laughter that resides behind their casual smile.

Night is the cloak that shields me, protects me from their punishing gaze, makes me feel like an equal, grants me the strength to believe that it's true.

All too soon it is gone, washed away by the light of a new day.

Once again, I am disfigured inside and out.

One day, I'll set myself free.

One day, I'll choose to walk in the sun.

Candlelight

Deep shadows danced around the flickering flame. One moment they were still; dark images cast upon a cold stone wall, the next, tormented spirits dancing silently to an incandescent tune.

He stared at the candle, watched the smokeless fire slowly consume the pool of wax forming around the base of the wick, then leaned forward and blew out the flame.

Darkness fell around him then. Only a tiny orange spark at the end of the wick stood out briefly against it. Before he could appreciate its fight, it was gone.

Darkness, this time complete, wrapped itself around him and drew him to sleep.

The Perfect Moment

His wife strolled to the window, her blue satin gown sliding from her shoulders to the carpeted floor.

He stared at her naked form, silhouetted against the light bleeding in through the blinds, then threw back the covers and joined her at the window.

"What a glorious sunset," he said.

"It's perfect." She reached out and clasped his hand. "I'm not sure I want it to end."

He bent down and kissed her neck, realising, in that moment, that he was the most content he'd ever been. He was finally at peace. All his young life he'd craved change, the years having passed so slowly, as to have seemed a prison. Now, ancient in the eyes of his children, he would have given anything to recapture those lost years.

He wrapped an arm around her slender waist and drew her close. Her head rested gently on his shoulder.

Now was not a time to long for the morrow.

Life and Death

I open the door to the crypt, but find myself unable to enter. I stand instead, transfixed by doubt, at the top of the stairs.

The faint hope that I'll find her still sleeping finally rouses me to action, and I descend into darkness.

As my eyes adjust to the gloom, my heart quickens, for I can see that my hopes have long since been dashed. The heavy stone slab that sat atop her tomb now lay broken upon the granite floor.

I scramble down the few remaining steps, silver crucifix and stake in hand, and peer into the empty silk-lined coffin.

A shadow flits across the open doorway and I turn to see my wife standing at the top of the stairs, her white skin pearlescent in the moonlight.

She smiles and beckons me closer.

Slowly, I ascend the stairs.

Though my heart is heavy, my mind troubled by the grisly task that lies before me, I know that I must find the strength to save her, for if I surrender instead to my truest desire, the embrace I crave will be my last.

Flash Fiction

Best Friend

The room is cold.

I'm waiting for Mother to come in from the living room to tell me that Max, our beloved dog, has passed away.

I've thought many times about rushing into the room and pulling the murderer away from my dog, imagining that he'll suddenly leap to his feet, bound over to the back door and bark to be let out, for there are games to be played.

Then I think of Max struggling to stand, struggling even to lift his head to the bowl, and I tell myself that this is for the best, this is the last gift we have to give.

Our life together, taken for granted for so many years, seems so finite now when counted second by second.

As I stand here, gaze fixed upon the window, I can think only of Max. The long energetic walks, the sprints through the forest, the play-fighting, full of life, with Father in the very room in which his life is now slipping away.

I hear the front door close, and I know that Max is no longer with us. Tears well and soak my cheeks. I hurriedly wipe them away as the door opens.

Mother stands there, her eyes swollen and red, tears streaking her makeup. She doesn't say a word, can't. Max is gone. She closes the door and the tears flow.

I've just lost my best friend.

Swimming Lessons

At the appointed hour, a hunched figure approached the bridge. Morgan was left with the distinct impression that the man liked black.

He wore a black leather trench coat, buttoned up to the chin, black gloves, black boots, and a large, broad-rimmed black hat.

The stranger made no sound as he approached, seeming to glide over, rather than walk upon, the cobbled stone.

As he stepped onto the bridge, his presence added weight to the darkness.

"You Carter?" Morgan asked.

The face inside the trench coat smiled, or at least Morgan assumed it was a smile. The top lip never moved.

"Heresy."

"What happened to Carter?"

"Drowned. A most unfortunate accident." Again, the tight-lipped smile.

Morgan glanced up at his companion, who shrugged. "Very well, *Mr. Heresy*. What can we do for you?"

"My client has a rather . . . unique problem," Heresy said, removing a small envelope from a pocket deep inside his coat, "one which he feels you would be willing to undertake, given the right incentive."

"A disposal job?"

"Yes, but there's to be no killing."

"No killing?" Morgan peered up at his companion once again. "Do we do that?"

"NOT KILLING'S EXTRA."

"It'll cost you five—"

"TEN."

"A further ten percent."

Heresy acknowledged the price with a nod, then handed over the envelope. "Try not to disappoint my client. He has a way of, shall we say, disappearing people."

"Is that a threat?"

A patchwork of emotions played across Heresy's face. After a few seconds of confused twitching, it seemed to settle on smug satisfaction. "Yes, I do believe that it is."

With that, the man turned and sloped away.

As he turned the corner onto Sword Street, the darkness receded and light leeched back into the city.

Morgan opened the envelope and read the letter. He then took a deep breath and peered over the bridge.

"I think," Morgan said, dropping a stone into the murky water and watching it sink to the bottom, "that now would be a good time to learn how to swim."

Saving the Galaxy

Commander Kray climbed the dais and received the adulation of the crowd. Large view screens, fixed to the glass ceiling, showed that the whole galaxy was watching.

"Ready, commander?"

Kray turned and saluted as the admiral of the fleet stepped forward and pinned the platinum medal upon his chest.

"It seems your heroic actions have once again saved the day, commander."

"Thank you, sir," he said, as the admiral shook him warmly by the hand. "Just doing my duty, sir."

The admiral stepped back, and Kray turned and waved once more to the cheering crowd.

He could hardly believe it. He'd finally done it. Flying the highly experimental FS-2 Starbird through the deadly Mintaran asteroid belt, he'd taken the mighty Vagraxian battle fleet completely by surprise. He'd then destroyed wave after wave of enemy ships to reach the Vagraxian home world and forced them to surrender.

The countless hours spent in the training simulator had finally paid off.

Of course, there'd been those who had doubted him, those who'd said he was wasting his time. He wondered what they were thinking now.

He was a hero, the saviour of Earth.

Now, if he could just save the galaxy from the evil inter-dimensional aliens, he'd become the greatest hero the confederation had ever known.

Kray knew they didn't stand a chance. After all, who was there now to stop him?

"Times up, commander."

Kray froze. Something cold and hard, like the barrel of a gun, was pressed firmly against his ribs. Slowly, he raised his hands . . . and removed the virtual reality headset.

His wife of eleven years was standing behind him. She was wearing a dry smile and held a spoon in her hand.

"Come on, you've had your two hours. Time to get off the computer. Your son has homework to do."

"But—"

She shook her head and glanced down at Tom, their nine-year-old son. He had that '*get off the computer, Dad*' look on his face.

Commander Kray sighed.

He knew he was defeated.

Saving the galaxy would just have to wait.

Harvey

I can't walk past the green gate at the end of my street without that black cat appearing.

He's only got half a face, and his right ear is missing. This was a cat that had already used up its nine lives.

I call him Harvey, but have no clue if that's his real name. Still, the name seems to fit.

I stop by the gate on my way to work every morning and scratch behind his ear.

One day, he doesn't appear.

I presume he's just late, so I wait by the gate for almost an hour.

The next day, I call my boss and tell him I'm too sick to come into work. I stay at home and keep checking the gate at the end of the street. He still doesn't appear.

I spend the rest of the week thinking about that bloody black cat.

I kept telling myself not to worry. I knew, deep down, that he was probably fine. I realised I was just saying these things just to ease my mind.

Twelve weeks later, I still have no clue as to what really happened. I still find myself thinking about that black cat from time to time.

Today my heart's feeling heavy, as I stroll down the street, towards the green gate where he used to wait. Much to my surprise, I catch sight of a familiar tail.

My heart skips a beat, and I find myself running to the end of the street.

That's when I discover that he is, in fact, she.

Tomorrow, I'll leave for work early. Harvey and her five coal black kittens will no doubt be waiting for me, beside the green gate, at the end of the street.

Mr Hennesey

A man in a tired grey suit was seated on the bench outside the park; a balding, middle-aged man, he wasn't at all what Hennesey was expecting.

He sat down on the bench and allowed his gaze to wander across the deserted playground. "You Cartwright?"

"Your ten minutes late, Mr Hennesey."

"Couldn't find a safe place to park, and it's just Hennesey."

"Well *Mr Hennesey*, I heard you completed your last assignment most satisfactorily."

Hennesey smiled. "It was easy, just like you said."

"Good." Cartwright licked his thumb and turned the crumbled page of his newspaper. "I want you to do it again, same street."

"What about my money?"

"You don't trust me, Mr Hennesey?"

"Trust must be earned, just like money."

Cartwright smiled. At least Hennesey thought it was a smile. The man's thin lips definitely twitched.

"I expect the job to be completed within the hour."

"And then I'll get paid?"

Cartwright stood and placed the paper he'd been reading into a florescent orange bag on the bench. "Don't disappoint me, Mr Hennesey."

Hennesey waited until Cartwright was out of sight before hefting the heavy bag onto his shoulder.

He was determined to do another good job. He needed the money. How else was he going to pay for the mobility scooter he'd be using to deliver all the papers to the houses on time?

Waiting

The streetlamp was a miser, apportioning light to the dark, rain-soaked street, like an English summer apportioned sunshine.

Harry was too tired to care. He slung his flimsy carrier bag over his shoulder and stared at the water gushing into the drain at his feet.

A piston engine roared, and he glanced up.

A beige Volkswagen pulled up onto the curb opposite and flung open a lime green door. A young woman in high heels stepped out, spoke briefly to the driver through the passenger side window, then ran, jacket over her head, into one of the flats opposite. A moment later the car growled away up the street, passing wind through its tail pipe.

Harry transferred his gaze to the darkened street. There was no sign of life, not even the faint hope of a distant car light.

He tore a hand through his rain-soaked hair, then hawked phlegm up from the back of his throat and spat into the street.

The wind picked it up, whipped it round, drove it back into his face. Scowling, Harry wiped the back of a muddied hand across his cheek.

"Bloody shittin weather."

His lips parted to form a lopsided grin that tugged at the sore on his lip.

At home, he knew his ear would now be ringing. Harry knew well the sound of one hand clapping.

He winced as his grin broadened. "Bloody, shittin, bloody, shittin, bloody, shittin, weather."

Turning his back to the wind, he pulled his numb fingers inside his woollen sleeves and thrust his hands beneath his armpits. He shivered violently, the glowing sensation it gave spreading warmth throughout his body.

He glanced at the clock hanging above the shop. Twenty to seven. He'd been waiting here nearly thirty minutes. Harry wasn't surprised. His father always seemed to lose track of time when he'd been drinking.

That's it, I'm walking home.

Harry didn't move. He had no wish to hear again the sound of one hand clapping.

So, he stood instead, staring bleakly at his trainers, feeling his toes squelch inside his socks, as the rain hammered the pavement at his feet.

Shell Shocked

Masterson heard his name over the thump and blare of the jukebox. He jolted upright and squinted at the reflection in the mirrored wall behind the bar. "Kenny?"

Kenny smiled and parked himself on a beer-stained stool. "Haven't seen the wife lately. She still sleeping with what's his name?"

Masterson ignored him and peered at the red-rimmed eyes staring up at him from the bottom of the glass. "Whatever it is, I can't help you, Kenny."

"What makes you think I want anything?"

"Because you're a leech," Masterson slurred, kicking back the dregs of his drink. "You exist to suck people dry."

Kenny's smile wavered, his fingers pawing nervously at his sweat drenched collar. "This time they mean business. They said they'd take my knee-caps if I didn't pay."

Masterson's brows rose an incredulous inch. "I didn't think you still had any."

"Look, I'll pay you back, you know I'm good for it."

Masterson whirled in his seat and shot Kenny a salted look. Kenny flinched as if stung. "You're one sick bastard, you know that?"

Kenny's face broke into a nervous grin. "Look, I'm sorry—"

"Like hell you are." Masterson swayed to his feet. He reached inside his jacket and threw a pistol onto the bar. It landed with a dull thud, the barrel pointing toward Kenny. "Chambers loaded, help yourself."

"Where are you going?"

Masterson smiled and pulled himself along the bar rail. "His name *was* Bishop."

"What? Whose name was Bishop?"

Masterson pulled his baseball cap low over his brow and staggered out onto the street. The smile dissolved as his fingers brushed the warm shell cases in his pocket.

Help Desk

"You've reached the help desk, Larry speaking. How may I help you?"

A voice on the other end of the phone breathes heavily into the receiver. "Can I speak to Charlie please?"

"I'm sorry, this is the help desk number. If you want to speak to someone in the department, you'll have to phone them direct."

"Okay. Can you give me their number?"

"4196."

"Thanks."

"No problem."

I put the phone down and lean back in my chair. Two seconds later, the phone assigned to 4196 rings. I dial ##3 and pick up the call.

"Good morning. How can I help?"

"Is that Charlie?"

"Charlie's not in the office right now. Can I help?"

"I have a problem."

"Okay," I say, "personal or work related?"

"Sorry?"

"Never mind, just a little light humour passing over your head. What seems to be the trouble?"

"My PC just crashed."

"Does it display an error message?"

"Yes." There's a long silence. "Would you like me to read it?"

"Sure. Go ahead." I pick up my pen.

"Okay. Here goes. An exception error at . . ."

As soon as I hear the words *exception error,* my ears go to sleep. I can't be bothered to stop the guy talking, so I glance up at the never-ending list on the job board. At the top, penned in bold blue ink, are the words:

WE RESERVE THE RIGHT TO REFUSE TO HELP
YOU

Nice idea, I think miserably. Shame we can't put it into practice.

". . . hello?"

"Sorry. Yes. Have you tried rebooting your PC?"

"I thought this was supposed to be the help desk?" The voice sounds peeved.

"It is."

"Well, I need to save the document I was working on."

What does the guy want me to do? I work in IT. I'm not a miracle worker. "Fine. Give me your name and department number and I'll add your job to the list."

I hear mumbled whisperings.

"Hello?"

Silence.

"Hello, can you hear me?"

"Yes."

"I need your name."

Silence.

"Charlie? Charlie? Is that you?"

I hear laughter and slam down the phone.

"Idiot." I wipe the job from the board and swear that's the last time I'll ever answer the phone for Charlie.

Charity

A grimy hand appeared out of the fog. "Spare a joey for a poor man down on his luck?"

Florence gasped and fell back, her heart pounding as she clutched the lace handkerchief to her chest.

The beggar was tall, his face pale and thin beneath a thick layer of grime, his oily black hair unkempt below a soiled grey cap. Thick, wide set brows sat above grey sunken eyes, and a dark scowl shaped the mouth under a heavy moustache, tearing at fresh sores upon his lip. A beard encrusted with soup jutted from an angular chin, revealing the contents of a meal that had been digested and most likely brought up again to make room for drink.

"How about a ha'penny then?"

The stranger moved to stand in front of her, not completely blocking her path, nor completely out of it.

His smile tightened, and she began to worry that the man would turn violent if she refused.

Hurriedly, she thrust her hand into her purse and withdrew a coin, a newly minted half-crown, and thrust it into his palm.

The stranger stared at it blankly, then lifted a hand to the peak of his cap and grinned. "God bless you, ma'am."

Squeezing a smile passed her lips, she hurried on.

At the end of the street, she glanced back and saw the shadow of the man fading back into the fog. She breathed a huge sigh and turned onto St. Thomas Street—where a sea of dark shadows now loomed.

What Might Have Been

I remember my last day of school so clearly it could have been yesterday. Hard to believe it had been twenty-two years.

Everything had changed.

After a particularly stressful day at work, I'll often find myself longing for the good old days—the days when mum would wave me off to the bus stop, when me and the girls would parade across the school field in our gym kit, acting for all the world like famous fashion models. Not that anyone paid us much mind. No one I knew was particularly popular at school.

Save, of course, for Billy Bragg.

The only problem with Billy, as far as I could tell, was his leech of a girlfriend, Melissa.

I hated her, and she despised me, crowing every chance she got, especially when she had Billy draped over her arm. To this day, I'm still not sure she ever loved him. She just couldn't bear to see him with anyone else.

On the last day of school, he gave me a goofy grin. He must have seen me blush, because the grin broadened into a smile.

Melissa retorted with an angry glare and whispered something in his ear. The smile died, and he turned away.

That was the last time I'd seen either of them, till today. They were married now, had three kids.

She was fat and sallow, her body rippling like melted ice cream beneath a blue floral dress. He was gangly, thin on top, and carrying a permanent scowl.

I smiled at him as they strolled past and saw the old light flicker deep inside his brown eyes. A sharp tug on his arm, however, and the light faltered and died.

I smiled to myself and continued walking. I guess not everything had changed.

Breaking Up

"What's the matter?" Peter asked. "You haven't said two words to me since we got on the bus."

Jane shrugged.

"It's the bangle," Peter said. "You don't like it."

"It's not the bangle." She forced a smile. "The bangle's lovely."

Peter grinned, and she squirmed inside. This wasn't going to be easy, for either of them.

"So, what do you fancy doing this weekend?" Peter asked.

"This weekend?"

"Yeah, I thought we could catch a movie or something."

I'll take the something, she thought miserably. She took a deep breath. It's now or never girl.

"Peter, I've got something to tell you, something important."

She looked down at the bangle, gently slid it from her wrist, and laid it on his thigh. He didn't look at it. He didn't need to. Her face was painting the wrong picture.

"Peter, I think we should stop seeing each other." There, it was done, said.

"No explanation, no reason, just like that." His eyes turned cold. "You've met someone else, haven't you?"

"No. I haven't. It's just . . . I need my own space for a while."

"And it's taken you, what, six months to work it out?"

She shrugged. "I didn't want to hurt your feelings. You 're nice and all, but—"

"Well, that makes it all right then, doesn't it," he said. "I'm nice, just not nice enough for you."

"You're twisting my words."

"Am I?" His gaze sharpened, and she shrank back from him. "What aren't you telling me?"

"Nothing."

The bus came to a stop, allowing an elderly couple onto the deck. They took the seat immediately behind them and for a while the pair lapsed into silence. Peter was the first to break it.

"How long have you been waiting to tell me this?"

"If I'm honest—"

"Oh, you can suddenly do honest. How refreshing."

"That isn't fair."

"Well?"

She glanced at him, then turned away. "About two months."

"Two months." Peter's lip curled. "You bitch."

"What?"

"Hyde Park, the concert, you just used me to get the tickets. That's why you didn't want to break up with me till now."

"God, Peter, is that all you can think about. I'll pay for the bloody tickets."

"I think I better go," Peter said, as the bus slowed for the next stop. "Before I do something stupid, like go out with you again."

Jane pulled in her feet to let him pass, then slid into his seat and stared out the window. She heard the bangle fall to the floor.

He bent down and picked it up, threw it on the seat beside her. "Keep it. When you're married and have kids, it'll remind you of the time you broke up with the guy who wasn't good enough for you."

He stormed down the bus aisle, took one final look at her, then stepped off the bus.

Jane slumped back in her seat, the tears flowing freely now, her thin shoulders heaving as she sobbed.

As the bus pulled away, she saw him slouch down the road and wondered, not for the first time, if it would have been simpler just to tell him she was dying.

Cheating

The teacher peered over the rim of his thick reading glasses. "You cheating again, Harris?"

"Sir?"

"Let me see your paper."

"My what, sir?"

"Your paper, bring it here."

Harris stood, cringing as the drawing pin driven into the leg of his chair scraped against the hard wooden floor.

"Quietly Harris, this is a test."

Harris strolled up to the front desk and slapped his exam paper on the table. He peered over the teacher's shoulder as his paper was being examined.

"What's the answer to question two, Harris?"

Harris's face flushed. "I don't recall the question, sir."

"Then allow me to refresh your memory." He reached into his desk draw and slapped a clean question sheet onto the desk. "The answer, question two?"

The room was silent. Harris stared at the question and allowed the silence to grow. When he was satisfied everyone in the room was listening, he said, "C, sir. The answer to question two is C."

There was a ruffle of papers in the classroom.

The teacher chose to ignore it. "And question four?"

"D, sir."

"Ten?"

Harris glanced down at the unmarked paper. "I believe it's B, sir."

The room was a flurry of activity. The teacher looked up, his gaze landing on a student with an eraser clenched firmly in his hand. "The next person to use an eraser whilst I'm talking to Harris is up for detention. Do I make myself clear?"

Twenty erasers bouncing off wood were answer enough.

He thrust Harris's paper back at him. "Why were you talking to Atkins, Harris?"

"He was mumbling, was all. I asked him to stop."

"Atkins?"

A small, grubby faced boy glanced up from his desk. "Sir?"

"Arse up here, now. And bring your paper with you."

Atkins grinned and marched up to the desk.

Apart from a few answers on Atkin's paper, the two were identical.

"Have you been helping Harris, Atkins?"

"No, sir."

"Why don't I believe you, Atkins?"

"Couldn't say, sir."

The teacher gave an exasperated sigh and leaned back in his chair. "Harris, take a seat up front where I can keep an eye on you. Atkins, return to your seat."

As Harris walked back to his desk to collect his things, he nudged Atkins with his elbow and smiled. "You get the answer you needed?"

"Yeah," Atkins whispered. "You?"

"Yeah."

"And stop talking," the teacher yelled, "or it's detention for the both of you, whether you're cheating or not."

The two boys grinned. Cheating was easy. All you had to do was ask the teacher for help.

Fat Lip

Cheryl slid the magazine across the table. "What do you think?"

Ken glanced at the header: *A New Face for a New You.* It was yet another article on cosmetic surgery.

The photo introducing the main article showed a woman in her late forties. Her skin was sallow and devoid of makeup. Her lips were thin and cracked, and her nose drooped slightly at the tip. She also had no definable neckline.

The picture reminded Ken of the turkey they consumed every year at Christmas.

The photo at the end of the article, if Ken could believe it was the same woman, had lost twenty years. The skin beneath her chin had gone, tucked away beneath a high shirt collar. The lines beneath her eyes had been stretched thin, the tanned skin, now replete with make-up, concealed any blemish. The surgeon had dotted every *i*, crossed every *t*.

They had erased all the character from her face.

"She's a dog," Ken said, turning back to his book.

"How can you say that," Cheryl said, taking back the magazine. "Did you even look at her?"

"Waste of money."

"You're only saying that to annoy me."

"Is it working?"

"No." Cheryl thumbed back the page of the magazine. "What do you have against cosmetic surgery, anyway? Everybody's doing it these days."

"I don't think you need it is all," Ken said.

"But if I want it?"

"I want Bailee Madison, but you don't see her hanging around here, do you?"

Cheryl smirked. "Not yet, no."

"Well then, either you're going to go through with it, or you're not. Either way, stop trying to justify everything to yourself through me, okay? You want to mess around with the way you look, fine, just leave me out of it."

"You're not going to try and stop me?"

"I'm sorry, did you hear what I just said?"

Cheryl grinned and leaned back in her chair. "I chose to ignore it."

"Fine. All I'm saying is that I can't understand why you'd want to put yourself through something like that. It's not even as though they could do much for you."

"And what's that supposed to mean?"

"It means half the girls in this library, heck, half the girls in this school would rather have your face." He turned in his seat and raised his voice. "Ain't that right, Charlie?"

A voice three shelves down, completely oblivious to their conversation, answered him. "Whatever you say Ken."

"See."

Cheryl smiled. "You know what Ken, you're the only person I know who makes me feel good about myself, it's why I'll never trust you."

"Trust me," Ken said. "Your nose is a little long, and shaped like a cumquat, but nobody cares."

Cheryl's face crumbled. "Who said anything about my nose?"

"You did," Ken said. "It's what we've been talking about, right?"

"No, it bloody well isn't," Cheryl said.

"Then what have we been talking about?"

"My lips," Cheryl said. "I was thinking about getting a collagen injection for my lips."

Ken smiled and stood up. His right fist struck his palm. "Hell, if all you wanted was a fat lip, all you had to do was ask."

New Faith

She was dying. There were no two ways about it. She'd been given six, maybe seven, months. Pancreatic cancer, they'd said. There was nothing that could be done.

She'd given up on life as soon as she'd received the devastating news. Now she spent all day in front of the TV. She'd planned to do so much with her life. Now all that was in ruins . . .

The doorbell rang.

"Who the hell could that be?"

She muted the TV and clambered off the sofa, the belt of her dressing gown trailing behind her as she slouched to the door.

A young man wearing a business suit stood on the welcome mat outside. His skin was luminous under the porch light. He smiled, and two pristine fangs protruded from beneath his upper lip.

"Good evening, madam. I'm sorry to disturb you at this late hour, but I was wondering if I might interest you in the new faith."

Great, that's all she needed, someone to save her. "Whatever you're selling, I'm not interested." She started to close the door, but his hand shot out, keeping it open.

"Come now, Cassy, are you so desperate to crawl back to your TV that you'd pass up a chance at salvation?"

She stepped back, and the door swung open. It wasn't so much what he'd said, or the way he'd said it. No. It was the use of her name that arrested her attention.

"I'll give you five minutes. But I warn you, if you're trying to sell me something—"

"Quite the contrary," the young man assured her. "I'm here to offer you something."

The man knelt and laid his suitcase on the ground. He opened it and took out a thin red pamphlet.

"Forgive me for asking," she said, "but . . . you are a vampire, aren't you?"

He smiled broadly. "Yes. I'm what you might call, recently deceased."

She reached out and took the pamphlet, then proceeded to thumb through its pristine white pages. "What exactly does this the new faith have to offer?"

"I'm glad you asked," he said. "But first, let me ask you something. Do you believe in God?"

She'd asked herself this question many times over the last few months. She'd even prayed a few times, hoping for a miracle. Either she wasn't trying hard enough or no one was listening.

"I'm not sure," she said at last.

"Very well. Do you follow any religion?"

She shrugged. "I always put C of E when I'm asked."

The vampire nodded. "A respectable and long-established faith."

"I hadn't really given it much thought," she said.

"Perhaps you should," said the vampire. "For instance, does your faith promise eternal youth?"

"No, of course not."

"What about immortality?"

Cassy shook her head. "No . . . well, I mean . . . I mean there's heaven, I suppose."

The vampire nodded, seemingly satisfied with her answer. "And have you been pious enough to get into heaven?"

Cassy folded her arms and gave a disgruntled sigh. "Look, I really don't see how—"

"Very well, for argument's sake, let's pretend that you haven't. What then?"

"I'm really not sure," she said. "Purgatory, maybe. I don't know."

"Now you begin to see the problem," he said. "People just don't know what they're getting anymore. Times have changed. People don't want to die old and lose everything they've strived so hard to attain. No. They want to stay young and enjoy the life they have now. They want results. They want guarantees. Am I right?"

"I—I suppose, yes, but—"

"Now, let me return to your original question," the vampire said. "What does my faith offer? I'll tell you. The Church of Modern-Day Vampires offers immortality, not in the next life, but in this one. And that's not some vague promise, that's our personal guarantee. Read the pamphlet and think it over. If you have any questions, my numbers on the back."

"I have a question."

"Yes?"

"Of all the houses in this street, what made you stop at mine?"

The vampire grinned. "Maureen, from the hospital's cancer support group, she asked me to call."

So that's how he'd known her name.

"She gave me your number, but under the circumstances I thought it best to call round in person."

"How did she—"

"A friend. One of the recently deceased. She said she couldn't live with herself if she denied you the same chance."

Cassy swallowed hard. "You mean she's—"

"One of us now, yes."

Cassy could scarcely believe it. If she took up his offer, she'd be able to do all the things she'd planned to do with her life. Hell, she could do a thousand things she hadn't even dreamed of yet. And if she didn't? Well, if she didn't, she'd be dead inside of five months.

Her heart raced for perhaps the last time.

"I don't need time to make up my mind," she said, thrusting the pamphlet back into his hand. "Where do I sign up?"

The vampire stepped forward and pressed two arched fingers onto the purple vein throbbing in her neck. "Right here," he said, smiling.

Janie

John opened his eyes and stretched till his joints cracked, then pulled the duvet back over his shoulder and stared at the brown leaf wallpaper. A television hummed in the background.

"You still think this wasn't such a great—"

John stopped talking. He gazed at Susan, his wife of eleven years. She was grinning at him. He smiled nervously. Where the hell was Janie?

"I can't believe I let you talk me into this," Susan said. "But now I'm here, now that we've actually done it, I want you to know, it was wonderful, every moment."

John continued to stare at his wife.

"What's the matter, wet dream?"

Perhaps that was it, a dream, a dream about Janie. That didn't explain why he was in a motel room, of course. It didn't explain why he'd just had sex with his wife, something he hadn't done in nearly three years. Nor could it explain how he'd enjoyed it.

"I need a moment."

"I'm not going anywhere," Susan said, sliding her foot up and down his thigh. She smiled, and something about that smile made him nervous.

He crawled out of bed and staggered to the bathroom, splashed cold water on his face. There was a reasonable explanation for all of this. He just needed to get to a phone, call Janie, and ask her what the hell had happened.

"What did I have to drink last night?"

"You don't remember?" There was a touch of humour in her voice.

He remembered squat. "I couldn't remember how much I'd drunk was all."

"You had no more than me, and I'm fine."

John peered round the door and stared at his wife. Susan had stopped drinking years ago, ever since she'd had the kids.

She caught him looking. "You coming back to bed?"

John's loins warmed to the idea, but his mind was still too preoccupied with Janie. He grinned.

"Actually, I was thinking about bacon and eggs." He towelled his face, then strode back into the bedroom, buck naked, and stretched out on the bed. Her fingers played along his chest.

". . . in the news today President Reagan has told the nation that he regrets the secret arms deal with Iran . . ."

"Why are they still going on about that?" John retrieved the remote from her side of the bed and turned off the TV.

"What are you talking about?"

"Regan. Eighty-seven. The arms deal. You remember?"

"Of course, I remember," Susan said. "It was on the news last night. Not really a morning person, are you John?"

"Last night?" John shook his head. "But that was eighty-seven."

He stared at his wife, noticed for the first time that her hair was cut short as in her youth, that her face had lost many of its characteristic frown marks. He drew back her side of the covers. Her body was smooth, athletic, not flaccid like he'd remembered. There was no scar running down her abdomen. "I must be dreaming."

"I work out," she said.

He smiled. If this truly was eighty-seven, then he hadn't met Janie yet. He wouldn't meet her for another ten years.

He ran his hand over Susan's firm stomach, felt her warm flesh tremble beneath his touch.

Not only that, he wasn't married yet. They didn't get hitched till eighty-nine.

His smile broadened.

Lloyd Honeyghan had lost his world welterweight boxing crown in eighty-seven. Alysheba had won the Derby, and Larry Mize the Masters.

John wasn't a betting man, but then, you couldn't really call this betting.

Short Stories

Betwixt Heaven and Hell

Harris reached down and picked up another stone from the embankment. It was large, about the size of his fist, and smooth where the rain of ages had moulded it, perhaps for just such an occasion. He slipped it into his corduroy trousers and set out again along the muddy track, shoulders hunched, head bowed against the rain.

"I'm cold."

"Yep," Harris said, turning up the collar of his Mac. "Being dead-e'll do that to ya."

"Dead?" The voice of the manslaughter victim, Joe Kipfer, echoed inside his head.

"Forgotten you were dead, huh?"

"Of course not," Joe said, touching Harris's cheek and forcing a perfunctory smile upon his lips.

Harris wiped the smile away and kicked open a herd gate leading off the trail. He glanced over his shoulder to make sure he was not being followed, then scrambled up onto the ridge overlooking the railway arches. Behind him, the gate slammed against its post housing, its ratchet tapping an eerie accompaniment to the wind rustling through the branches of the willow and birch trees overhead.

"So, where are we going?" Joe asked.

"I told you already, for a walk."

"Long walk."

"Yeah, well, I got a lot on my mind."

"Not so much," Joe said.

"Meaning?"

"You can't keep secrets from me."

Harris grinned and pushed back a mop of hair. "I got secrets."

"Not from me, you haven't," Joe said. "Suicide, right? You're thinking about jumping off the old rail bridge."

"Clever bastard, ain't ya?" Harris said, bending down to pick up another stone. "Now, stay the hell out of my thoughts?"

"Sure, I can do that," Joe said.

But even as he spoke, Harris felt Joe padding through his thoughts once again.

"But tell me, where would the fun be in that?"

Harris opened his mouth to offer rebuke, but instead sucked in the cool night air. He focused on driving Joe out of his mind. He might as well have tried spooning his thoughts. An explosive sigh escaped his lips. The wind caught and discarded the white vapours of his breath. Frustrated, he kicked the toe of his boot into the gravel, sending a shower of stones down into the cutting.

Harris felt his lips twitch, but held off a smile.

Joe was getting stronger, gaining control. A few more days, perhaps a week, and Harris knew his mind, his very soul, would be set adrift in his own body.

It was a disquieting feeling, one that had driven him to this final, desperate act. The bridge, having loomed large in his mind, now loomed large over the brow of the hill.

Harris stopped and took a deep breath. Seeing the bridge had brought home what he was about to do. His troubled mind recalled the day of the accident.

It was a late December evening. He'd been drinking. He'd thought about calling a cab, then decided against it. He hadn't drunk that much. Not really. He could still drive.

Then the cyclist had appeared, seemingly from nowhere. He'd slammed on the brakes, but it was too late. The cyclist sailed over the car bonnet and hit tarmac. Harris hit the accelerator and sped away. He glanced in his rear-view mirror and saw car lights in the distance. After that, he didn't look back. He hadn't even known if the guy was dead or alive.

Three days later, Joe came to him in a dream. At the time, he'd thought nothing of it. It was the shock of the accident. His unconscious mind playing tricks. Only later, when Joe started speaking to him, did he start to doubt his sanity.

Since then, Joe had grown from a whisper, locked away in some dark recess of his mind, into some sinister force capable of manipulating his thoughts and actions. Like it or not, Joe was now a part of his psyche.

These dark thoughts, and Joe's humming of Chopin's Funeral March, carried him to the bridge.

"I don't think this is a good idea," Joe said, as Harris approached the railings.

"What's the matter?" Harris delighted in the idea that Joe was frightened. "Don't fancy dying again?"

"I was thinking of you. Hell, why should I care if you jump?"

"Because you know that when I die, you'll die too. You only exist because I do. You think I haven't figured it out, but I have. You've been playing for time. Well, guess what? Time's up."

Harris swung his legs over the railing and gazed into the murky waters of the river. At first glance it appeared to be black ice, but a sick yellow foam riding the water, swirling round the stanchions beneath the bridge, told him the river was fast flowing and swollen from the recent rains. His face paled and his stomach cramped. He was suddenly afraid, and he didn't care if Joe knew it.

"Last chance," Joe said.

Harris ignored him and glanced toward the distant city. Its lurid lights, once burning brightly, now struggled to attain adequate shades of grey. Joe, having turned Harris's world into a dishcloth, had wrung out all the colour.

"My God." Somewhere, deep inside Harris's mind, Joe smiled. "You're really going to do it."

"Goodbye, Joe."

Harris raised his arms and leapt off the bridge. The brief flight was exhilarating, the cold air rushing past his face, whipping back his hair. So, this was what it was like to fly, he thought. And then he had no time for thought.

He hit the glassy water, the impact jarring the air from his lungs. He gasped for breath, but the dark water swirled around him, dragged him down. Water and silt escaping the river filled his lungs.

Panic roused his limbs to action, and he struggled to break the surface, but the current proved too strong, wrenching him under until he could no longer see the light of the rail lamps playing on the surface.

A feeling of emptiness, black and oppressive, followed.

And for a time, there was nothing.

Then a light, brilliant and unyielding, appeared, and when he opened his eyes, he gazed out across a vast white expanse.

He was standing in a long line, one of hundreds that stretched out as far as he could see, along paths furrowed into the clouds. It was summer here and a pleasing warmth fired his limbs. In the distance, a large white gate topped with trumpeting angels glistened.

Further along the path, away from the gate, a grey-haired angel dressed in a plain white suit dispensed tickets to the bewildered masses.

Harris turned. Again, the white expanse stretched on without end. Every few seconds, someone materialised in line behind him. Dressed like him, in a simple white cotton chemise, they stood in quiet confusion, looking lost and, despite the multitude, alone.

A gentle tap on his shoulder caused him to start in alarm, and he spun round. The angel dispensing tickets stood before him. White mist swirled at his feet.

The angel handed him a ticket and started to move on. Harris grabbed his arm and squeezed. "Where am I?"

The angel smiled but said nothing.

Harris gave him a violent shake. He drew back, startled when a white feather fell from unseen wings and floated on past the floor.

"Where am I?"

"Betwixt Heaven and Hell," the angel answered calmly.

"I don't understand."

"Harris Leech died. You now await judgement. Heaven, or Hell."

Harris shook his head. The name sounded familiar. "I don't remember."

"That's as it should be." The angel pointed back along the path just taken. "When your number is called, walk up to the gate."

Harris glanced at his ticket. It was thin and shiny, like gold leaf, and had the number 651 stamped upon it. "Who will judge me?" he asked.

The angel did not answer. Instead, a voice, soft and disembodied, called out to him.

"That would be me."

Harris wasn't sure, but somehow he knew, in another life, he'd heard that voice before.

Supermarket Express

I slide the seat belt off my shoulder and glance into the rear-view mirror. My daughter Teai is slouched in the back seat.

"Come on," I say. "Let's get it over with."

She glares at me, unaware that I'm watching. "I'd rather wait in the car."

Here we go again, the same thing every week. In a moment she's going to provide me with an excuse for not helping with the weekly shop, something lame like toothache. Inside I'm fuming; outside I'm as calm as a summer day.

A red exercise book spins through the air and lands on the front passenger seat. I pick it up and flick, uninterested, through several pages of French scrawl.

"What am I looking at?"

"Homework."

I catch a deep-seated sigh and clench my teeth. Grasping the plastic steering wheel, I slowly squeeze the blood from my fingers.

Since when has Teai been interested in homework? As far as I can tell, she's only interested in two things, boys and nightclubs. Homework is her excuse, her way of wheedling out of her promise. Well, not today. Today she will help, even if it kills her.

"No dice," I say, throwing the exercise book onto the back seat.

"But—"

"But nothing," I snap. "Out."

She throws herself at the door, glaring at me in defiance as she jumps out.

Cringing as she slams the door, I struggle out of the car, swing my handbag over my shoulder and chase after her, catching up to her at the trolley park.

"Come on," I say, forcing a smile. "It won't be that bad."

Her scowl doesn't agree with me. She snatches a trolley and scrambles through the sliding glass doors.

I close my eyes and perform a few breathing exercises.

Friday night shopping is always the same, one argument after another. All I want is some help around the house, but Teai isn't receptive to that idea. Getting her to help has proved impossible, so I made her promise to help me with the shopping every Friday after I get home from work. It's a promise I'm determined she'll keep, even if it drives me mad in the process. No matter how hard I try to avoid it, we always end up arguing.

When I open my eyes, a sympathetic shopper smiles at me. I return his smile and enter the supermarket. Teai is waiting for me, her gaze trained on the checkout.

"Grab yourself a magazine," I say as we pass the magazine rack. "It will give you something to read on the way home."

"I've got homework, remember?"

"Something to read over the weekend then."

She ignores me.

"What the hell is wrong with you?" I ask.

"Nut'en."

"It's pronounced 'nothing,' and there must be something. Your bottom lip is raking dust off the floor. I'm surprised you haven't tripped over it."

"It's noth-ing, okay?"

"No, it's not okay. You haven't said two words to me since we've got here. Tell me the truth and don't give me any lip about homework."

"Fine," she says. "You really wanna know?"

"Well?"

"Why does everyone else get to go out on Friday nights, but I have to go shopping with you?"

"Is that all?" I scoff.

"What do you mean, all? Isn't that enough?"

"For Christ's sake, Teai. You're sixteen. Doesn't that mean anything to you? God knows you don't do anything at home. Don't you think it's time you took on some responsibility?"

"Like Dad, you mean?"

I grab hold of the trolley and wrench it from Teai's hand. "Go wait in the car."

"Fine."

The following Friday, we're shopping again.

Half way down the frozen aisle section, Teai suddenly stops the trolley. I direct my attention to the boy stacking shelves.

I glance at Teai. She looks nervous. "New boyfriend?"

"Mark Bradley. He works here most evenings after school." She starts to walk towards him. "I'll catch you up, okay?"

"Fine, just don't get him fired," I say, teasing.

She turns to me and smiles. "Not much chance of that."

"So, when do I get to meet him?" I ask Teai later that evening.

She peers at me over the rim of her mug. "What do you mean?"

"You and what's his name, at the supermarket."

"Whatever made you think I could be interested in him?"

"I thought—"

"He already has a girlfriend. And no," she says, seeing me about to ask another question. "I'm not interested in him that way."

"What other way is there?" I ask.

She pauses to consider her answer, biding her time by wetting her lips with coffee. "I was thinking about what you said last week, about taking on more responsibility."

I lean forward and seat my elbows on the table. She is being serious. "And?"

"I asked him if there were any jobs going at the store."

"And?"

She smiles. "I have an interview next week."

My first thought is to wish her luck. My second thought is to question her motives. "This isn't your way of telling me you're not getting enough pocket money, is it? Because––"

"Mum."

"What?"

"I'm trying to tell you that I'm sorry. Ever since Dad left, I realise I've been a pain. Instead of helping you, I—" She waves aside the rest of her comment. "You didn't need that. I've decided to take your advice. I've decided to grow up."

What can I say, I'm stunned, not only by the fact that she's apologising and putting herself forward for a job, but that she asked a supermarket assistant. Why hadn't she looked at the job vacancy board like everyone else? What did she hope to accomplish by speaking to him? My confusion is evident because she laughs, spilling a mouthful of coffee into her mug.

"Don't worry, Mum. He's the store manager's son."

Two weeks later, I'm spending my first Friday evening at home. Teai got the job at the supermarket, working three evenings a week. Now she does the shopping and I get a free local delivery service.

The front door slams. I rise from the kitchen table and walk over to the sink to fill the kettle. Moments later, Teai staggers into the kitchen and swarms the table with shopping.

"Can I help?" I ask.

"It's okay. I got it," Teai says.

"Tea?"

"Please, I'm exhausted."

As if to emphasise the fact, she slides onto a chair and flops forward onto the table. When I turn, I'm surprised to see forty pounds lying on the table.

"What's that?"

"Housekeeping. I thought you might need it, for emergencies and stuff."

I slide it back across the table and smile. "You've earned it." And for once she has.

"I better get changed," she says.

The money stays on the table.

I watch her walk upstairs, then stare at the bags of shopping on the kitchen table and smile. She still hasn't learnt to put the shopping away, but I'm working on it.

John Dory

The constant taunting, the name calling, the hurtful comments concerning her birthmark, Cally learned to endure. The tactless remarks about her clothes, a selection of grey knitted jumpers and worn grey-suit trousers, she chose to ignore. Even the repeated trips to the changing rooms for a quick shampoo in the girls' toilets, she accepted as just another part of the Monday morning ritual. But what tormented her, what made her heart bleed every time she heard it, was the nickname Chad had given her at the start of the school term.

"John Dory," Chad's voice boomed, drowning out the chorus of voices in the hallway.

Cally's heart faltered. Blood pounded her temples. She searched for a friendly face in the hallway, desperate to avoid another encounter with Chad, but came away empty. As Chad approached, she glanced away, wanting nothing more at that moment than to dissolve into the crowd.

"Need a word," Chad said.

"Really? Right now?" She sounded cheerful, but her feigned effort succeeded only in widening the leer on Chad's face.

"Right now."

He took her arm and marched her to the nearest classroom, slamming the door behind him as he swung her round to face him.

"Now, tell me, what the hell are you playing at?"

"P—playing?" Cally stammered. "I don't—"

Chad swiped the desk with a tatty exercise book. She flinched, her legs trembling inside her grey-suit trousers. "This is what I'm talking about."

"Your English assignment?"

"Is that what you call it?"

Cally's hands clenched and unclenched nervously at her side. "I didn't think it was that bad."

"Not bad? She gave me a D-, for Christ's sake. A stinking D-. Hell, I could have done it better."

"Then why didn't you?"

"Because that's your job," Chad said, "or have you forgotten?"

Cally shook her head. She hadn't forgotten.

He smiled and caught hold of her wrist, pressing his body against hers and inhaling her perfume like she was the butt of one of his cigarettes. His gaze flicked across her crimson birthmark to the leather satchel slung over her shoulder. "Open it."

For a moment she thought she might refuse, but the smile on his face, broadening into a grin, made her think twice. She threw the satchel onto the desk and stepped aside, watching as he rummaged around inside and began drawing objects out onto the desk.

"No condoms, no smokes. Jeez, what are you? The virgin fucking Mary?" He threw everything back into the bag and slung the satchel at her.

"That mean I can go?" Cally asked.

"You can go when I say you can—"

Before Chad could finish, the classroom door opened. Billy Carter stood in the doorway.

"You okay, Cal?"

"She's fine, aren't you, Cal?" He wrapped an arm around her thin shoulder and laughed, an unpleasant guttural sound that rattled the phlegm at the back of his throat. It was midmorning and already he reeked of cheap beer and cigarettes.

"Cally?" the voice piped once more from the doorway.

"I'm fine. Really."

She hated having Billy see her like this. Not that she wasn't always glad to see him. Billy was the only true friend she had, but he didn't need to see her humiliated like this.

"Well, I hate to break up whatever it is you two have going," Billy said, "but there's a class starting in here in two minutes. You might like to take your business elsewhere."

Chad snorted, gave her shoulder a painful squeeze, and recovered his assignment. "Be seeing you, John."

Cally cringed and glanced at her shoes to hide her flushed cheeks. Her body, white from staying in from the sun, began to warm to her embarrassment. Sweat pooled beneath her armpits.

"What's with the John?" Billy asked, after Chad had gone.

"He thinks it's funny."

"I don't get it."

"Neither do I," she lied.

It was only after she'd learnt that a John Dory was a fish with over large lips that the name had any effect on her. She had always considered her lips to be the only redeeming feature of her face. Now Chad had taken even that away from her.

"I wouldn't worry about him," Billy said, squeezing her arm gently. "He wafts through this school like a bad smell. You sure you're okay?"

"I'm sure," she mumbled. "Thanks."

When Chad stepped out from beneath the stairwell at school the next day, Cally wasn't surprised to feel her heart lurch in her chest.

"Where the hell you been?" he said, "I was about to come looking."

"You wouldn't have found me."

"I'd have found you. Girls' toilets, behind Mr Gray's office, right?"

Her cheeks flushed in response.

Chad grinned. "That my assignment?"

"Yes."

"What'd I write about?"

"The Secret Service. Best read it before handing it in."

He snorted. "Yeah, right. Straight after I get that hole in my head." He flicked through the foolscap pages, squinting at the text. "Any good?"

"It should be."

"Damn right it should." He ran his finger down the margin of the last page. "What will she give me," he said, referring to Miss Hatcher, the history teacher who would be marking the assignment. "C, C+?"

Cally shook her head and looked up at Chad through the tangled mass of red hair that had fallen across her face. "After yesterday I thought—"

"Thought what? You trying to be funny?"

"I thought you wanted an A. I was up half the night finishing that assignment."

"You're shitting me, right?" Chad's gaze narrowed dangerously. "You better be shitting me."

Cally shook her head in lieu of stammering.

"What the hell you playing at? If I hand this in, I'll have to stand up in front of assembly and collect me one of those damn bookworm certificates. I'll be screwed."

Cally's nervous smile brought him to a halt. "And if you don't hand it in?"

Chad's eyes flared. "I can kiss goodbye to my lunch break. I suppose you think that's funny. I suppose you think you've got one over on me."

"I've decided I don't really care what you think anymore," Cally said. "You see, it's not my problem. It's taken me until now to realise it's been yours all along."

"And what's that supposed to mean?"

"It means I'll continue to do your assignments for you, but every time you hand them in, you'll be expected to stand up in front of assembly. I've decided you're going to become the school's biggest egghead. How long do you think it'll be before people start asking you to do their homework for them? A month, two? You're not the biggest bully in this school, believe me."

"And what's to stop me beating on you anyway?" Chad said, clenched fist revealing "HATE" penned onto his white knuckles.

"Miss Hatcher. She has no idea I've done all your assignments to date. She would do if I told her. You've been bullying me for what, nine months? You fancy taking all those assignments again?"

He grabbed her wrist and squeezed.

"Get smart, Chad," Cally said, squeezing the threat past the tremor in her voice. Something brought him to his senses because her arm slid through his fingers. "I'd say you've got a lot of thinking to do. Should be a new experience for you."

"Bitch."

Cally ignored him.

"Before I go, I want you to know something. That assignment you're going to hand in. I didn't write it. I haven't, in fact, written any of the assignments you've given me. Do you understand?"

Chad shook his head.

"John Dory did."

"You're John Dory," Chad said thickly.

"Not me," Cally said, with the ghost of a smile. "I'm Cally, Cally Jones. Remember?"

Her smile broadened into a grin as she turned and walked away, making her way slowly toward the green exit sign and home.

She was no longer John Dory. From now on she was and always would be, Cally Jones.

Berbalang

Alfred opened the front door of his bungalow and peered over the rim of his reading glasses. A young woman in a pink polyester jumper stood there. "Yes?"

"Abigail Walters. I phoned from the university."

"You did?"

"Last week, my thesis . . . imaginary friends, remember?"

"Ah, yes—"

"You did say I could come round?"

He frowned and glanced at the clipboard and the backpack slung over one shoulder. "You a student?"

"Afraid so."

"I thought you'd be older."

"What can I say?" She smiled, her feet shuffling on the cord mat just outside the door. "Sorry to disappoint?"

He unhooked the chain securing the front door and waved her inside. "Who said I was disappointed?"

He tied a loop in the cord of his dressing gown as she wiped her boots on the mat, then closed the door and followed her into the living room.

"Tea?"

"Tea would be lovely," she said. "Thank you."

He waved her into a chair beside the electric fire mounted into the ingle, then stepped down into the kitchen, steadying himself on the sloping guide rail screwed to the parquet wall. The water in the kettle was already coming to the boil.

He snatched a cup from the cupboard and placed it on the worktop beside his own. "So, you're studying for a degree?"

"A Bachelor of Science in Psychology."

"Sounds . . . interesting."

"Not really. It's what I need to become a Clinical Psychologist."

Alfred grinned. "Fruit loops."

"Excuse me?"

"Mental patients," Alfred said. "You want to work with mental patients?"

"People with special needs, yes."

He poured boiling water into the cups and gave the tea bags a quick stir. "And this thesis of yours on imaginary friends—it's part of your course?"

"It's part of my chosen field of study, yes."

"And what about old duffers like me?" Alfred returned to the living room, tea tray in hand. "Where do we fit in?"

"Recent studies have shown that there are as many elderly people with imaginary friends as there are children who claim to have them," Abigail said earnestly, watching Alfred ease himself into his chair. "Though I tend to think children put them to better use."

She smiled as she said the last, her youthful exuberance allowing Alfred to glimpse the woman beneath the make-up. Alfred's lips mirrored a tremulous response. Only where her smile was bright and breezy, his seemed tired and worn, ineffectual.

"Well, I'll have to take your word for it. You're the expert, after all, not me."

"I'm only a student. I—"

Alfred shook his head and waved her to silence, setting his glasses down on a pile of old newspapers stacked beside his chair. "Sure, you are. A few more years and they'll be calling you a fellow."

"Don't say that. Please." She affected a sigh.

Alfred slumped forward, offering her a selection of biscuits from a tin he'd been surprised to find still in date. "Sorry. Didn't mean to offend."

"None taken." She glanced over the selection, took one, then placed it on the saucer beside her cup.

"Just the one?"

"I'm watching my weight."

Alfred didn't doubt her claim. The woman was painfully thin, only recently out of her teens, with pale skin and pronounced cheek bones. What she really needed, he thought, was three square meals a day and as much pudding as she could stomach.

"Shall we get started?"

Alfred gave a terse nod, then glanced down as she crossed her legs, his gaze caught between her black leather skirt and black square-toed boots.

"Perhaps we could start with your friend's name," she said.

"I call him Berbalang. Don't know his real name. Don't care to either."

She started writing, faltered, then looked up from her notes. "An unusual name?"

"I suppose," Alfred said. "I got it from one of those whatcha-ma-call-it magazines." He clicked his fingers in the hopes of recollecting the name, but this time he was out of luck.

"Probably not important," she said. "What can you tell me about him?"

"Besides the fact he's an imp, you mean?"

"Really?" She flicked back through her notes. "I'm pretty sure I have a gremlin here somewhere. I don't suppose it's the same thing?"

Alfred's face eased into a smile. "Yes and no."

"Perhaps you could describe him to me?"

"Where to begin?" Alfred mused. He then followed with a description of Berbalang that ran to a full page. When she'd finished writing, she looked up.

"He sounds—interesting."

"He's a pain in the proverbial. I'm sure it's not the same thing."

"So why do you put up with him?" she asked.

"Oh, he has his uses." Alfred paused and took a meaningful breath, casting his gaze around the room. "Mind if I ask you a question?"

"Shoot."

Alfred cleared his throat. "Most people assume I'm, you know, a little crazy, because I have an imaginary friend."

"Understandable."

Alfred's keen expression faltered.

"It doesn't mean they're right, of course."

"Quite." He paused to consider his question. "What would you say if I told you Berbalang was real? I mean, as real as you or me?"

She'd obviously been asked this question before because her answer came swift and without hesitation. "I'd believe you believed he was real. And at the end of the day, that's all that really matters, isn't it?"

"I—I suppose." It wasn't the answer he'd been hoping for.

"Besides, I collect them," she said, a half-hearted smile drawn out on her lips. "So, what does that make me?"

Alfred didn't answer. He smiled and allowed his gaze to wander once more along her thigh. This time, she caught his gaze and her face flushed. She smiled weakly and gave her skirt a sharp tug. If she had a tick box for dirty old man, he knew she'd just ticked it.

"Is Berbalang with us now?"

"No. He disappeared as soon as you arrived."

"You don't find that at all suggestive?" she said, in what Alfred imagined to be a Freudian tone.

"I'm old, not senile."

He watched her make a florid mark on the page.

"And how did you acquire your new friend?"

"Hard to say. He just turned up one night while I was asleep. I believe it was late summer because I had the window open. I heard a noise and when I woke up, there he was, hanging on the curtain, glaring down at me."

"Glaring?"

"I got the impression I wasn't supposed to see him. He seemed to take offence at the fact. After I'd switched on the light, I watched him fling himself against the open window, but he just seemed to bounce back against thin air."

"And when he'd finished trying to escape?"

"He sat at the end of my bed, staring at me with those large grey eyes, puffing away on a cigarette."

"And what was he doing? In your house, I mean?"

"Stealing."

Her eyebrows raised in question.

"All my valuables," Alfred said. "Anything that was small and glittered."

She nodded studiously as she reviewed another page of information, then looked up. "And how long has he been living with you?"

"About three years. Three years ago, last week, my wife passed away. It's how I remember."

"I'm sorry," she said, "I didn't mean—"

He waved her sympathy aside, it being all anyone offered these days. "It wasn't a happy marriage," he said simply. He glanced at the tea still on the table, now cold and swimming with the fat of the milk. "Aren't you going to touch your tea?"

She smiled uneasily and pressed the cold cup to her lips, straining the tea through her teeth. "Very nice," she said, "thank you."

He smiled politely, despite the fact she didn't lie very well.

"Your friend," she said, returning the cup to the tray almost immediately, "is there anything else you'd like to tell me about him?"

"Well, for starters, you can stop calling him my friend," Alfred said, in a voice that was little more than a whisper. "He's more of an acquaintance, really. We just sort of put up with each other. Probably thinks he can outlive the old coot and escape."

"Escape?" Abigail asked in a low voice, adding to the effect of Alfred's already conspiratorial whisper.

Alfred nodded and leaned closer. "He can only leave the bungalow if someone else enters in his stead. Then, as soon as they leave, he's forced to return. I get the impression he can only truly escape when I, you know." He rolled his eyes toward the ceiling.

"Pass on?"

"Exactly." Alfred was about to say more when he caught the look of concern on her face. Talking to an old man about death was obviously making the young woman uncomfortable. He let it drop.

She ceased writing and stabbed her pen into the paper, forming a full stop on the page. "I think that's everything."

"No more questions?"

She glanced at the clock on the mantelpiece and shook her head. "I really should be going." She slung her backpack up onto her shoulder. "I've still got two more people to interview today."

"Two more crazy people?" Alfred asked.

"No," Abigail countered. "Two more imaginatively gifted people."

He laughed at that and the phlegm riding the back of his throat gurgled. He sounded like an old tractor in need of spark plugs and an oil change. "I won't argue with the expert."

He showed her to the front door and clasped her hand.

"It's been a pleasure," she said.

"For both of us, I'm sure," he said, resigned to the fact she was now leaving.

He smiled and waited for her to close the gate at the end of the drive before shutting the front door and returning to the living room. He sank into his chair and stared at the smoke–stained wallpaper above the mantelpiece, now shimmering like a ripple on still water.

A moment later there was a cork–popping sound and a small grey-scaled creature flew out from the wall and landed, uncerermoniously, legs splayed, against the nook of the chair arm.

The creature appeared dazed and peered up at the old man, as if struggling to bring him into focus. When its eyes finally widened in recognition, a half-smile twisted its thin lips.

"Pleasant trip?" Alfred asked, snatching a small pouch from the imp's grasp.

Thin, cracked lips, stretched over small white fangs, produced a hiss of displeasure. "What do you think?" the imp retorted hotly, back-pedalling along the chair arm out of harm's way, beyond Alfred's reach.

The old man glanced at the imp, then threw his gaze to the chair opposite. "Make yourself comfortable, why don't you?"

The imp flew across the room and circled the soft cushion like a cat, snuggling down into the warm spot vacated by Miss Walters. A moment later, Alfred waved aside cigarette smoke in order to view the collection of jewels displayed on the table.

Alfred's brow furrowed. "No stones?"

"What did you expect?" the imp replied indignantly. "Fine jewels?"

"One can but hope."

The imp shook its head, its lips drawing back into a half–baked smile. "She was too young, not even married."

He'd known that as soon as he'd seen her. She'd not been wearing any jewellery.

"She sounded older on the phone."

"How much older?"

"Meaning?"

The imp raised its hands in mock surrender, then clasped them firmly behind its head, propping its feet up on the chair arm. "How many more pigeons do you have lined up this week?"

Alfred consulted a small black diary and read out the first two names. "Shirley Staines, from the 'Friends of the Aged.' She'll be here on Tuesday, and Mrs Saunders from the 'PTA,' who'll be here on Friday."

"Old birds?" the imp asked.

Alfred ignored the imp's sarcastic comment and clambered out of his chair; his gaze trained on an old tin perched on the mantelpiece. It was full with the jewels he'd collected over the three years since Berbalang had been stealing for him.

Abigail Walters would doubtless return home to discover she'd been burgled. She would no doubt file a report with the police. They would search for clues and find nothing. No fingerprints, no signs of forced entry. And the neighbours? They would have seen and heard nothing, like all good neighbours should.

"The perfect crime," Alfred said, cradling the tin in his arms. "And all it took was a little imagination."

Heaven's Calling

In 1929, England won the third test against Australia. The Supermarine Rolls-Royce S6 won the Schneider Trophy. And the liner Bremen made the eastbound Atlantic crossing in a record 4 days, 14 hours, and 30 minutes.

In 1929, Jack Gumble died.

He was standing in a plush hotel lobby. Symphonic jazz was playing over the radio. White marble gleamed floor to ceiling.

An angel behind a reception desk glanced up from his crossword and unfurled his wings. The downy feathers ruffled in the breeze of the ceiling fan. "Welcome to the Grosvenor Hotel, sir."

Jack ignored him and glanced around the marble lobby, his gaze affixing to every detail. When he was satisfied that he didn't have a clue as to how or why he was here, he turned back to the angel behind the desk. "How did I get here?"

"You don't remember?"

Jack shook his head.

"I shouldn't worry, sir. It will all come back to you. For now, however, if I could just have your ticket."

"My ticket?"

"Yes, the one you received at the gate."

Jack glanced back at the revolving glass door that led out onto a street paved with stars. "I didn't pass through any gate."

"No gate and no ticket." The angel brushed a loose strand of hair from his suit. "Why, it's a wonder you arrived here at all."

"Which brings me back to my original question," Jack pointed out.

"Yes, well, I guess we should probably establish where you are first. Or have you already figured that part out for yourself?"

"Of course."

The angel relaxed.

"This is the Grosvenor Hotel."

The angel forced a smile. "I'm afraid this is merely a facade, a fabrication we've plucked from your subconscious mind to assist with your transition."

"My transition?"

"To the afterlife."

"You're trying to tell me this is heaven?"

"Think of it more as an annex to heaven, a waiting area if you will." The angel flexed his wings as if to make a point. The gesture was lost on Jack. His mind was too busy wrestling with an uncomfortable fact.

"But that would mean I'm—"

"Yes. I'm afraid so."

"But I don't feel dead," Jack said.

"Ah! Yes! But have you ever been dead before?"

There was an irrefutable logic to the question, one that deemed any response from Jack rather mute. I mean, how did one go about checking if they'd died before?

"Tell me, what's the last thing you remember?"

Jack thought long and hard about the question, then smiled. "I was playing cards, poker. Yes, I was playing poker."

"And?"

The smile faded. He remembered clutching his chest and falling, falling so hard the table collapsed. There were voices calling to him. Everything went black, and then . . .

"But I can't be dead," Jack insisted. "Look at me, I've never felt more alive."

He stared into the oval mirror hanging behind the reception desk. He was wearing a grey striped lounge suit, a plaid blue necktie, and a straw boater hat. His face was clean-shaven, with a strong chin, and a nose that was a little too long and roman for his liking. He couldn't have been more than what, thirty, thirty-five?

The angel peered at a clipboard on the desk and ran a finger down a list of names and addresses. "It says here that you're a Mr. Jack Gumble, recently of 57 Larkin Way."

"It does?"

The angels' heavy eyebrows piqued. "It also says that you shouldn't be here."

"See, what did I tell you."

The angel shook his head. "I think you misunderstand. Your reservation, it was cancelled."

"My reservation?"

"Everyone is born without sin, Mr. Gumble, ergo, everyone has a place reserved for them in heaven. That reservation is only cancelled if some transgression is made. You don't really think we'd allow just any Tom, Dick . . . or Jack into heaven, do you?"

"I—I suppose not." Jack's mind raced because his heart no longer knew how. He pulled at his starched collar. "May I ask why it was cancelled?"

The angel flipped through several sheets of paper. "According to this, you were a gambler and a womaniser."

"Really?" Jack sounded surprised. There's no way he would have considered himself handsome. He must, therefore, have been rather rich.

"I'm afraid so. On August 19th, 1923, you committed adultery."

"So, I made one stupid mistake—"

"The first of many, I'm afraid."

"Really?" Jack grinned. "I must have had a hell of a life." The grin faltered. "I don't suppose I have time to repent my sins."

"Traditionally, that's something you do before you die. It rather makes a mockery of the whole process if you get to do it afterwards."

Jack shrugged. They'd been no harm in asking.

"It also states that you're an atheist, Mr Gumble."

104

"Yes. I mean no . . . NO . . . that was before."

"Before?"

"Before I met him," Jack said, surprised that he'd forgotten.

"Him?"

"You know, the big man upstairs."

The angel flashed his Duraglit teeth at Jack. "God is not open to house calls, Mr Gumble." He slid a pen and a form across the desk. "Please read and sign the reverse to say that you've understood the terms and conditions of your release."

"Release?"

"We're letting you go, Mr Gumble."

"I don't understand."

"I have no option but to send you back. Reincarnation is the only viable option left open to you. Until you can learn to live a sin free life, I cannot allow you to enter heaven. Looking at your resume, I could see about sending you back as any animalia, perhaps a lower primate?"

Jack wasn't liking the sound of this. "And if I don't want to go back?"

The angel smiled, but it was no longer benevolent. He tore a stub of paper from the bottom of the consent form and released it above the floor. A spiralling flame immediately leapt up and consumed it. Jack's gaze trailed the burning ember to the floor. Hurriedly, he picked up the pen and reached for the form.

As his pen touched the page, a golden ticket fluttered briefly in the air and came to rest upon the desk. It was an I.O.U.

Jack Gumble, having been proved worthy of admission, is forgiven all past sins and transgressions, and permitted free, unrestricted access to the heavens.

The angel's blue eyes widened.

"What can I say," Jack said, strolling toward the glass doors of the casino, "God's one lousy card player."

Death by Habit

LeFanu, justice of the peace for the shire of Bardsley, stood outside the Prior's locutory in Callway Abbey and awaited the summons of Prior Albinus. Though he was the law and above the banalities of peasant life, it did not do to upset the holy orders. Even with the law on his side, he knew it could not always be counted upon where the church was concerned. LeFanu, after all, only had the ear of the King, and even he had to answer to God.

When the summons finally arrived, it was an hour after matins, the first of eight daily services set aside for prayer.

"You are Henry LeFanu, justice of the peace for this shire?" inquired Prior Albinus softly.

"I am."

The Prior's thin lips exercised an uneasy smile. "Thank you for coming to Callway Abbey."

"I am here because the law demands it," said LeFanu. "Now if you would tell me, how does my presence here best serve the King's Peace?"

The Prior's smile faltered. "This morning Brother Crandall was found dead in his cell. Our Master of the Infirmary suspects suicide."

"But you did not summon me here for that?"

The Prior shuffled uneasily in his seat. "There is a more disturbing possibility."

"The possibility of murder?"

"This is what I need you to discover."

LeFanu acknowledged this with a shrift nod. "I have been assigned quarters?"

"In the dormitory."

"The law also demands that someone bear witness to my findings."

"Brother Temman will attend to your needs."

LeFanu bowed stiffly to the Prior. "Tell me, is Brother Crandall's cell close to mine?"

"It is. Why?"

"That is where I shall begin my investigation."

Brother Crandall's cell was a cubicle of grey stone. Light, permitted entry through a tiny cross-slit in the south wall, produced a small cross that would sit directly above the bed at sunrise. A pine wood cot, doubling as a bench, sat in the far corner, opposite a table and chair, the latter of which now lay on the floor. Two shelves, laden with jars, sat above the table.

LeFanu observed all this from the doorway, his sharp gaze examining everything in the room. Two things immediately stood out in his mind: the herbs forming a pile at the right leg of the table, and the abundance of herbs left half crushed inside the mortar.

LeFanu turned to Brother Temman. "Who discovered the body?"

"Brother Aelfwig."

"And where is he now?"

"In his cell, awaiting your summons."

"I see. Did anyone else see the body prior to its removal?"

"Only myself and Prior Albinus," Brother Temman replied.

"And what was your general impression?"

"I concluded that he must have overdosed, but by accident or design, I cannot say."

"And what, specifically, led you to this conclusion?"

"The mortar he used to mix his herbs," said Temman. "It contains a vast quantity of his sleeping draught. I recognised one of the components. It was cowbane."

LeFanu was impressed. "At what time did Brother Aelfwig discover the body?"

"When Brother Crandall did not show up for Matins, Brother Aelfwig was sent to wake him."

"This was a usual occurrence?" LeFanu asked.

"No. Only when he'd taken his sleeping draught did he occasionally sleep overlong."

"I see. And at what time did he retire to his cell?"

"Eight of the clock, after Compline. He was then required to attend Nocturns, which he did."

"Was that the last time anyone saw him?"

"It was."

LeFanu nodded and peered once more around the room. "Other than the body, has anything in the room been touched?"

"No. Besides myself and Brother Aelfwig, only the Prior has entered this cell. Once the body was removed to the infirmary, the door was locked and a message sent to you at Rhileworthy."

LeFanu's gaze swept back to the table. "The herbs Brother Aelfwig used, he had an intimate knowledge of them?"

"He assisted the Master of the Infirmary," said Temman. "I cannot say more than that."

"Then I shall ask no more on the matter."

Unable to learn more without entering the room, LeFanu cautiously stepped inside. Brother Temman continued to hover by the doorway.

"Where was Brother Crandall when you found him?"

"On the floor, there," said Temman, pointing.

"By the table?"

"Yes. He was lying on the ground. His face was bloated, his limbs similarly distended."

"A succinct description," said LeFanu, stepping over the chair. He took the mortar from the table and rubbed his fingers into the crushed herbs. His nostrils flared as they drew in the smell. "You mentioned cowbane——I concur. It is one component of the sleeping draught you mentioned. I also detect sweet cicely, but there is something else."

LeFanu remained silent a moment. "Tell me, did Brother Crandall suffer from the falling sickness?"

"I do not think so. Why?"

"It would help explain the presence of hemlock." He tipped the contents of the mortar onto the table and gathered some of the herbs from the floor. The tips of his fingers itched. "I will need some boiling water."

Brother Temman returned from the kitchen some ten minutes later. "What shall I do with it?"

"Pour a small amount into the mortar and leave the rest on the table."

Temman did as instructed, then stood back. The sweet-smelling vapours wrapped around LeFanu's face.

"An interesting combination," LeFanu said, placing the mortar back on the table and dipping his fingers into the bowl of warm water. "Horehound and ipecac." He wiggled his fingers inside the bowl. "The smell is quite unmistakable."

Satisfied with the herbs' genera, LeFanu turned and looked for something to wipe his hands on. Seeing only Brother Temman's habit, he dabbed his fingers on his own woollen shirt and stepped forward to examine the herb jars.

He counted twenty-two in all of various shapes and sizes, all made from the same thick glass. Three jars stood out, not because they were different, but because they were set apart from the rest, claiming fully half the top shelf. They had no labels, but showed signs of having had them. He reached up and removed the jars from the shelf.

He then sat a moment in reflection, the fingers of his right hand worrying his bottom lip. Why had the herbs, one an emetic, the other an antidote for poison, been discarded on the floor? It certainly did not befit the act of a dying man. Why had the mortar contained enough cowbane to kill a stable full of horses? And why had three jars been stripped of their labels when the others were so meticulously kept?

Certain the answers did not lie inside this room, LeFanu sprang to the door and looked back at the startled face of Brother Temman. "It is time we questioned Brother Aelfwig."

They found Brother Aelfwig seated on his cot, face buried in his hands. He looked up as they entered, his face worried with questions.

"Brother Aelfwig?" LeFanu asked.

"Yes?"

"I would like to ask you a few questions regarding the death of Brother Crandall."

"Am I then a suspect?"

LeFanu brushed the question aside. It was his job to ask questions. "Tell me, why would someone want to kill Brother Crandall?"

"Then you believe it was murder?" Aelfwig's pallid skin achieved a nervous sweat. He passed a trembling hand over his tonsured head.

"It was a hypothetical question," LeFanu said, putting up a hand to forestall further questions. "Now, if you would answer the question."

The Brother bowed a nervous apology. "I doubt any here in the Abbey could give reason for his death."

"Very well. Tell me, as a Lay Brother, what were his duties?"

"Manual labour, mostly tending the herb gardens and administering to the sick in the infirmary. He took great pleasure in both."

LeFanu nodded and stared directly at Brother Aelfwig, his sharp gaze drawing in every aspect of the Brother's face, from the thick, black crown of hair on his head, to the nervous twitch of his lips. Brother Aelfwig seemed to quail beneath the look.

"Cicta virosai, you know what it means?" asked LeFanu.

The Brother drew a deep breath as if testing his lungs for the first time, then spared his tongue the trouble of forming a coherent sentence by shaking his head.

"Cowbane," said LeFanu. "It is the Latin name for the herb you placed in Brother Crandall's mortar."

"I——I," Brother Aelfwig flustered and wiped a black sleeve across the sweat pooling on his forehead. "But—— but how?"

"Prior Albinus assured me that nothing in Brother Crandall's room had been disturbed. The room presents evidence to the contrary. Therefore, you, as the first on the scene, must have done so. What the evidence cannot tell me is why?"

Brother Aelfwig's face flushed crimson. He reached down and removed a piece of cloth from inside his habit, and held it out to Brother Temman.

"What is it?" LeFanu asked.

"A handkerchief," said Temman, "covered with blood."

"I wiped that from his lips," Aelfwig said, voice trembling. "Had I known he'd been murdered——"

"Why touch the body at all? Why not simply report his death to the Prior?" LeFanu asked.

Brother Aelfwig dared a furtive glance at LeFanu. "I did not want his soul to suffer long in purgatory," said Aelfwig. "The taking of a life, especially one's own, is a terrible sin, an affront to God." He looked up at LeFanu, but this time held his gaze. "I could not sit back and let that happen. I had a chance to do something, I took it. In life, Brother Crandall was a man of Cardinal virtue. He should have been accorded no less in the hereafter."

Aelfwig's confession made sense, even if his actions served only to cloud the issue of Crandall's death. Aelfwig had wanted to make Crandall's presumed suicide look like a simple accident. He might have succeeded had he been given time to dispose of the evidence so hastily discarded on the floor. It also explained why he needed to remove the traces of blood from Crandall's lips. An overdose of cowbane would not have elicited such a response.

LeFanu lifted a jar from his purse. "Tell me, did you lift the label from this, or any other jar in Brother Crandall's cell?"

"I did not," Aelfwig said, genuflecting innocence. "I——"

A bell rent its fury on the air.

LeFanu questioned Temman with a look.

"The Nones bell," said Temman. "The monks are required to attend church at this hour."

LeFanu nodded understanding. "Then now would be a good time to examine the body."

Brother Holt, Master of the Infirmary, was waiting for them.

He was tall and well built, but his habit did not disguise the fact that his muscles had long since run to fat. His coarse linen robe, taken up by his broad shoulders, was too short and drifted loosely about his ankles. His grey tonsure, having followed the robes example, had receded into a thin crescent. His face, imbued with life, of a colour and depth only associated with wine or strong mead, produced a wan smile.

LeFanu extended his hand and felt it grow moist inside Brother Holt's meaty palm. "Henry LeFanu, justice of the peace."

"Prior Albinus said to expect you."

"Then I can assume you have had plenty of time to prepare your answers," said LeFanu. "Tell me, how many patients have died in the last week?"

Brother Holt looked surprised but did not balk at the answer. "Three."

LeFanu raised an eyebrow. "So many?"

"Several villagers from Boarfield were recently struck down with the bloody flux. Most of the victims were escorted here. Few are likely to recover."

LeFanu accepted this without further comment. "And of the three who died, how many were from the village?"

"All three."

"The bodies, they're still here?" LeFanu inquired.

"All three remain in the mortuary. It is customary to wait seven days before burial."

"I see." LeFanu's expression grew grave. "Would it be possible for you to re-examine those bodies?"

"If I knew what I was looking for?"

"Poison." LeFanu drew the unlabelled jars from his purse and held them out to Brother Holt. "I need you to match these to any you keep in store."

"But don't you want to ask any questions about Brother Crandall?" Brother Holt asked, as LeFanu walked away.

LeFanu turned. His thin lips painted a hot-glass smile. "Let me know when you've finished examining the bodies."

LeFanu spent the next two hours in muted conversation. The patients in the infirmary, all of whom Brother Crandall had administered to at one time or another, spoke of a man most pious in his duty.

LeFanu stood and prepared to talk to the next patient when a Lay Brother stumbled into the infirmary.

"Brother Holt would see you in the Locutory," said the Lay Brother, wheezing like a man forced to draw breath through a straw.

"Did he give his reasons?" said LeFanu.

The Lay Brother shook his head. "He said only that you were to come immediately."

"Then let us not keep him waiting."

A few minutes later LeFanu was speaking to Brother Holt in the Locutory, a small room set aside for monks who wished to indulge in private conversation.

"Your assumption was correct," Brother Holt said gravely. "At least two patients were poisoned."

"Two?" LeFanu echoed softly.

"I have not had time to prepare for a proper examination of the third."

"Very well. Have you been able to ascertain the nature of the herbs from which the poisons were derived?"

"Better than that," Brother Holt said. "I can name them for you."

"Indeed?"

"Hemlock and mandrake."

"These herbs, they came from the jars I provided?"

"It hardly seems credible."

"Nevertheless," said LeFanu.

"It's possible."

117

"Tell me, was Brother Crandall the only person, besides yourself, with access to these herbs?"

"No. Any Lay Brother who was required to tend the gardens would have had access."

LeFanu nodded, satisfied with the answer. He bowed to Brother Holt, then turned to leave. He made it as far as the doorway. "One more question. Did any of the patients display signs of hematemesis, vomiting of blood, before they lapsed into coma?"

"Yes, the last." Brother Holt sounded surprised. "Is that important?"

"Indeed," said LeFanu, only vaguely aware of the question. His mind was already lodged deep in thought. "You have been most helpful."

LeFanu spent the next half-hour in silent contemplation. When he was ready to report his findings, Prior Albinus did not keep him waiting.

"Brother Temman informs me you are ready to leave," said Prior Albinus. "Does this mean you have been able to ascertain the truth?"

"It does."

"And?"

"I believe Brother Crandall was murdered. Moreover, I believe that three of the patients from your infirmary were also murdered."

At these last words, the Prior's face paled. He exchanged a glance with Brother Temman, who, after a swift nod of acknowledgement, dutifully lowered his tonsured head. Even with the Brothers' affirmation, LeFanu wondered if the Prior, whose face had now regained much of its colour, would be inclined to dismiss his findings and motioned toward the door.

"Brother Holt can be called upon to confirm my findings."

"Your word will suffice for now," the Prior said, waving the comment aside. "Please continue."

"I learned that Brother Crandall had been in the infirmary a few hours before he died. He had apparently been comforting a dying patient. I believe Brother Crandall and this patient ingested the same poison."

LeFanu fumbled inside his leather purse for the bottle and placed it on the table.

The Prior's gaze did not waver.

"What is it?"

"A rare herb imported from the continent."

"And you believe this herb was ingested by Brother Crandall?"

"I do."

"And where did you acquire this herb?"

"The room of Brother Crandall."

LeFanu expected the Prior to protest but instead received only a gentle inquiry.

"You said murder. Now you imply suicide."

LeFanu shook his head. "I believe Brother Crandall administered the poison to the patient."

Prior Albinus, now displaying no outward sign of discomfort other than a piqued eyebrow, guided the bottle to the edge of the table. "Why would a man of the church, a man who has dedicated his life to God, suddenly bed the Devil?"

"I deal in facts," LeFanu replied with a gesticulation of his hand. "Anything else leads to supposition. All I can do," he said, "is present you with facts."

"Then pray do."

"Mandrake, Hemlock, and Gourd. The names are familiar to you?"

"Herbs used in the infirmary," said Prior Albinus.

LeFanu nodded. "True. Mandrake, when mixed with poppy and vinegar, is a powerful anaesthetic, and by itself an emetic. Hemlock, like many poisons, has antidotal properties when administered against another poison. I site strychnos nux-vomica, or Dog button, as an example. Brother Crandall used these herbs because they were readily available and fairly safe to administer. And because they were already in use in the infirmary, they would have aroused the least suspicion."

"So why use Gourd?" Prior Albinus asked.

"The effects of mandrake and hemlock are well known. I suspect Brother Crandall wanted to see what effect a relatively unknown herb, such as Gourd, would have."

"A supposition?"

LeFanu conceded the point. "It has been a long time since I read Avicenna's Canon Medicinae, but as far as I am aware, Gourd carries no medicinal properties."

"What you say makes sense," Prior Albinus said. "However, I cannot condemn a man's soul to purgatory on your say so."

"Nor should you. Brother Crandall's room also contained three bottles that had been set aside from the rest. They were also the only bottles stripped of their labels. We know that two patients died from poison, from two of the three substances contained in these bottles."

"If what you say is true," the Prior murmured, drawing hastily upon the evidence, "it still doesn't explain the murder of Brother Crandall."

"The last patient to be poisoned received a lethal dose of Gourd. I believe he knew, or at least suspected, that he had ingested poison and through some sleight of hand ensured that Brother Crandall ingested it too."

"And just how did you arrive at this conclusion?" Prior Albinus asked.

"The patients told me that Crandall was a man of peculiar habit. During the late hours of Compline, he would choose a patient and sit with him through to Nocturnes. I believe he was actually observing the poison at work. When he later retired to his room, he began to observe those same symptoms in himself. There is evidence at a hurried attempt to concoct an antidote."

"The horehound and ipecac we found on the floor beside the table," said Brother Temman.

LeFanu acknowledged this with a swift nod. "Horehound is a powerful anti-agent, though I have had little opportunity to measure its effects. The ipecac would have been used as an emetic."

"So, it was murder," Prior Albinus said softly.

LeFanu made a deprecating motion with his hand and strode toward the door. "I would much prefer to call it justice."

The Beast of Hunting

Eadbald stumbled into the clearing and reached for the bough of a nearby tree. A branch bowed against his weight, snapping back violently as he swayed clear, sending a shower of snow down from the heavily laden branches. Drawing in a deep breath, he leaned back against the broad oak and looked out across the snow-covered heath.

"Why am I here?"

Eadbald sighed and closed his eyes, clenching a fist to his tired brow.

Because he needed to be.

Despite the cold, despite the pain, despite the weary journey that had seen him slog five miles through the deep snow, he needed to be here.

Reluctantly, he pushed away from the tree and followed the snow-laden path up the hill toward the ramshackle building.

A few minutes into the climb, his body warmed to the task, and his lungs rasped against the cold morning air. A cry sounded from the low valley, and he stumbled in his haste to discover the cause. Falling backwards into the snow, he cursed as fresh pain flared across his back. A crow, evicted from its roost by the high winds, flew overhead, uttering protest.

Eadbald shook his head and returned the sword, half-drawn from its sheath. Perhaps it was just the beast preying on his mind that had him so on edge. There was certainly nothing in this feral landscape to warrant concern, nothing that could not be bested by steel.

Cresting the hill, Eadbald approached the dilapidated hut, struggling to quell the tide of fear swelling up from the pit of his stomach. Something outside the purview of his senses, some primeval instinct for survival was screaming in his ear, telling him to run.

Run.

Eadbald balked at the idea.

He had seen Oswulf's body on the herepad, had seen, first-hand, the destruction wrought by the beast. Tears welled and melancholy threatened. Eadbald shook off the memory.

No. He would not run.

Running would accomplish only one thing—another night of brutal madness.

Cautiously, he climbed the broken steps, the wood bowing to accommodate his weight, then put his shoulder to the door. The warped wood gave way, and he stumbled inside.

The stench of rotting flesh and fetid decay hit his nostrils, and he recoiled as if struck. Bile rose and touched his lips, and he scrambled outside.

Mouth dry, he hawked phlegm up from the back of his throat and tried to swallow, but vomit lodged and warmed the back of his throat. He bit down on his lip and drew blood, then hawked the contents of his stomach over the stair rail.

When the nausea had passed, he turned his face to the wind and drew in the cold morning air, then returned to the doorway. As his eyes adjusted to the gloom, a fresh wave of panic threatened to drive him, not only from this place, but from the low valley he called home.

Blood had spun a furious web over the wattled walls, forming dark pools in the woven straw. Bones, human and animal, robbed of flesh and marrow, were strewn about the floor like some giant perversion of the 'pick-a-stick' game he'd enjoyed as a child. Animal excrement, mixed in with the straw, formed narrow valleys on the hut floor.

A small table and a three-legged stool were seated beneath a shuttered window by the south wall. A conical prism, lying on a warped shelf above the table, dissected the early morning light peering in the through shards of broken glass. A leather tome sat on the table; beside it, a quill pen and ink.

Eadbald stooped beneath the door lintel, shoving shards of bone aside with his boot as he headed for the table. His back to the door, he eased himself to the stool and flipped to a random page near the back of the book.

Woden's eve, 59th day of summer in the year of our lord 897AD

This day, Edgar de Banwyrhta has been appointed our local Catchpole. I don't like him. More to the point, I don't trust him. Dorvald de Maestlingsmid, a man of good reputation, and a retired Fyrdsmen of twenty-five years should have been appointed to the position.

Sun's eve, 70th day of summer in the year of our lord 897AD

Hardin is born to Raizel and Godric. I am honoured to accept the role of Godparent. I have asked Freeland to fashion a shawl from the red broadcloth I acquired last week.

Moon's eve, 1st day of autumn in the year of our lord 897AD.

The carnival is up at Hunstable again. I could not be persuaded to go. Several days later, I am told a wild beast broke free of its cage and mauled several bystanders.

Eadbald stopped reading. A hastily scribbled wolf's head was depicted in the margin of the next page. Scanning the journal, he found several more entries scattered throughout the text. Having found what he'd been looking for, he turned back and read the first wolf marked entry.

Frig's eve, 12th day of autumn in the year of our lord 897AD.

My heart raced today for the first time in twenty years. I was making charcoal in the wood up by Eachann's oak when I heard Acca scream. I grabbed my hunting knife and dashed through the forest. Making for the stream, I spotted Acca on the far bank. A huge dire wolf was chasing her through the trees.

I took up a heavy stone and threw it at the wolf. It was a lucky throw, the stone striking its flank. I expected it to run. Instead, it bounded across the stream and bore me to the ground, its slavering jaws snapping at my face.

Face pillowed to the earth, I raised my knife and plunged the blade deep into the wolf, caring not where I struck.

The wolf shuddered, then collapsed, its massive weight anchoring me to the ground. Its slavered breath remained hot upon my face.

I confess, I would have wept with relief had Acca not suddenly appeared at my side. In that moment, I felt live again, for I had slain the beast and lived to tell the tale.

Acca praised me to heaven.

Today I am the most celebrated man in the village.

Bad fever in the night.

Sun's eve, 21st day of autumn in the year of our lord 897AD.

The injuries sustained rescuing Acca from the wolf have all but healed.
I am in good health. Carei said I looked sixty again. She always did
have a wicked sense of humour.

Father Maccus believes I must have received a divine blessing for
my injuries to have healed so quickly. He tells me that I can best show
my appreciation by way of a small remuneration to the stave church.
Now I don't know what to believe.

Dorvald is trying to pair me off with a woman from a neighbouring
village. I tell him I am too old to take on a wife.

The next passage recounted the diarist's recent good
fortune and Eadbald pressed on to the next wolf scribed
entry. He found it several weeks later.

Moon's eve, 36th day of autumn in the year of our lord 897AD.

A wild animal has killed all the chickens up at Wiglaf's farm.

I am reminded of the wolf that attacked Acca some three weeks
earlier. It had been half crazed with hunger. Life is harsh for man or
beast.

Edgar searches the high pastures, but he's no tracker. He returns
at nightfall empty handed.

Tiw's eve, 37th day of autumn in the year of our lord 897AD.

Worril drove his cart to Bishlop today. He swore blind that something in the woods on the east side of the croft was watching him. Rather than return to the village, he spent the night at Bishlop.

Woden's eve, 38th day of autumn in the year of our lord 897AD.

Young Akly is missing. A search party scoured the pastures and woods surrounding the village, but could find no trace of him. His mother fears the worst.

I would sit with Holli to keep her company, but my own dreams are strangely troubled of late.

Thunor's eve, 67th day of autumn in the year of our lord 897AD.

The foul beast has struck again, this time closer to the village. Three sheep slaughtered; the rest panicked into the low valley.

A hunting expedition is assembled outside the Great Hall. What I wouldn't give to have twenty years of my life back to hunt the beast.

Four days have passed since poor Akly went missing. I hold little hope for his safe return.

Frig's eve, 68th day of autumn in the year of our lord 897AD.

Conwulf is dead. He was a thief and a womaniser, so I cannot say he will be sorely missed. The manner of his death, however, is something

I would not wish upon any man. I have seen to it that the horrific circumstances of his death, and the events leading up to it, do not go undocumented.

The day began with Modig reporting Conwulf's disappearance.

Edgar organised a small search party. We searched the woods and the roads leading out of the shire before widening the search to include the curving shoreline.

Braiden found him in a small cut-away by the harbour. His face drained of colour, and he waved us back. Staggering from the body, he dropped to his knees and heaved the contents of his stomach up onto the dewed grass.

Later that night, Braiden told me that the right side of Conwulf's face had been completely torn away, and that his ribs had been splayed open to provide access to the organs beneath.

There is no longer talk of wolves.

Cynric has sent Aldin to fetch the local farrier. I remind him that the nearest town is thirty-five miles away; two days by oxcart.

Today I shall pray that Odin's law protects the sanctity of the village.

Saturn's eve, 69th day of autumn in the year of our lord 897AD.

Oswulf is found dead on the herepad, his ribs splayed open for all to see.

It was a grisly sight, made all the more terrifying by the fact that I had spoken to him but an hour before. I shiver at the thought that it could so very easily have been me.

Tracks are found in the tithe barn. I speak to Dorvald later that day and he informs me that the beast had probably lain in wait, perhaps for several hours, before choosing its victim. It is a chilling proposition and one I care not to put about the village.

The villagers arm themselves by day and lock themselves away at night. I pledge earnestly to do the same.

Sun's eve, 70th day of autumn in the year of our lord 897AD.

Edgar, our much-exulted Catchpole, is nowhere to be seen. Goneld and Strayga say he is still out tracking the beast. I know better. He has fled to the relative safety of the town.

I feel we have good reason to fear. Yesterday, all the hounds in the village fled. The days are eerily silent.

Dorvald is made village Catchpole.

Eadbald squared his aching shoulders and stared into the gloom. The day was waning fast and his tired eyes now strained to read the text. Rising from the stool, he searched the byre and found a stub of tallow candle. Its cheerless light flickered feebly against the growing dark.

Frig's eve, 73rd day of autumn in the year of our lord 897AD.

The Farrier has not arrived and Aldin has failed to return. I doubt he would stay up in town with his wife and child still here in the village. Fears run high for his safety.

Sun's eve, 75th day of autumn in the year of our lord 897AD.

Found and buried Akly this day.
   It is small comfort, but six days have passed without incident.

Frig's eve, 9th day of winter in the year of our lord 897AD.

Megan is dead.
   Death is visited upon us again this day.

Saturn's eve, 10th day of winter in the year of our lord 897AD.

Freya is dead.
   The village is now rife with talk.
   Strayga claims to have seen a wolf that walked upright with the gait of a man. No one dismisses her claim. Though she caught only a glimpse of the beast, silhouetted against the light of the full moon, she described in some detail how it sniffed the air before loping into the woods at the far end of the village.
   Her words fill me with dread, for she has spoken aloud that which has haunted my dreams of late.

132

Tonight, I plan to chain myself to the beam above my bed. I have procured a sturdy chain from the bronze smith for this purpose. If the night passes without incident, and I pray to the Almighty that it does, I shall know the truth of my condition.

Sun's eve, 11th day of winter in the year of our lord 897AD.

Woke to the sound of a fist pounding on my door. I got up to find Dorvald standing in the doorway. His face was ashen, his expression dire.

I didn't need him to tell me what had occurred. Everyone in the village is summoned to the Great Hall. The sturdy chain that was to have been my salvation lies broken at the bottom of my bed.

Knowledge, my once trusted friend, now sits on my shoulder like the proverbial devil. I am trapped, not by the foul infection that has robbed me of my humanity, but by the knowledge I have gained, the knowledge I would now give anything to dispossess, for knowledge has driven all hope from the path set out before me.

Eadbald sighed inwardly and stared into the smoking flame. His heart hammered against the silence. Reverently, he turned the page and took up the quill, scraping the nib across the crisp vellum.

This morning, I set out early from the small village of Hunting to slay the beast that has, for too long, slaughtered the innocent of our village. For months, it has fed on our fears and sated its hunger amongst our kin. Only now, when the beast's true nature is revealed, can I finally act.

His hand began to tremble, and he eased the quill away from the parchment, unwilling to allow his emotions to sully his work. When the moment had passed, he dipped the quill back into the ink, scratching the nib along the rim of the inkwell before returning the pen to the page.

This day, in the year of our lord 897AD, the Beast of Hunting was slain by my own hand. So ends the horror visited upon us. I pray to the Almighty that its like never finds us again.

He discarded the quill and stared through the slats in the window. Long shadows raked the earth as the winter sun hankered below the treeline. The purple sky, now full of dark clouds, slowly inked its way to black. Time yet to fulfil his promise.

Unsheathing his dagger, he pressed the pommel against the table ledge. The silver point pricked his skin, drawing a rivulet of blood that ran the length of the blade. Then, mouthing a silent prayer, he blew out the candle and drove the blade deep into his chest.

A scream, half-man, half-beast, tortured his throat. He felt the power of the beast ride him, felt his blood course, inviting the change. But it was too late. The beast could no longer save him and he had not the strength, nor the will, to save himself.

Conclusion

I hope you've enjoyed the stories in this book and that they've left you with a desire to keep reading. If they have, I heartily encourage you to do so. With so many wonderful books being published each year, you can be sure you'll never run out of good things to read.

If you enjoyed this book, please consider leaving a favourable review on Amazon. This not only helps support my work, but motivates me to keep writing. Thank you.

Printed in Great Britain
by Amazon

12175816R00079